# TWELVE GRAVES OF CHRISTMAS

## A JANE LADLING MYSTERY
### BOOK FOUR

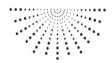

## GENA SHOWALTER
## JILL MONROE

Cover Created by Leni Kauffman

Editing by AZ Editing

Proofreading by Naomi Lane

The following images through CreativeFabrica.com:

Chapter Header: PadmaSanjaya

Ornamental Breaks: CRStocker

Prologue and Epilogue Header by julynx through Depositphotos.com

This book is dedicated to all our furry friends!

# PROLOGUE

## Cattain's log

*December 25th, Year 2 a.j. (After Jane)*

$\mathcal{T}$he invader has encroached upon my territory again.

His name is Conrad Ryan. And yes, his daring is commendable. But I do not commend him! He is such a fool-hardy human. How can he not know I, Cattain Rolex Ladling, am not a feline one trifles with? Not without conse-quences, anyway. I am royalty! His Royal Highness the King of Dead Mouse Court, Prince Of Cattitude, Duke of Purry, Earl of Mayhem, Baron von Murder Mittens, Royal Knight of Clawsovenia, Distinguished Member of the Order of Whiskerus Maximus, Grand Master of the Furian Empire, Guardian of Disorder, Royal Chief of Chaos, Lord Raven-death of the Garden's Most Honourable Kitty Council, Personal Aide-de-Camp to Her Majesty's Slightest Whim, and Lord High Admiral of Bughuntland. My rage knows no bounds!

Though I've attempted to slay the scourge with my glare two hundred thirty-three and a half times today, he has somehow survived.

I hunger for vengeance. I thirst for his pain.

After I complete my six-to-twelve-hour evening nap in the bowl on the kitchen table, grab a quick snack, assassinate a feather, cough up a hairball, knock over a vase, and perform a total body licking, I will ensure he regrets being born.

He should be quaking with fear. I've already sharpened my claws.

The usurper deserves only misery! He has ruined Christmas for me and my servant-queen, Jane. I've done everything in my immense power to remind her of happier times without the male. Stared at her unblinking for endless minutes. Removed annoyingly shiny orbs from our new indoor tree. Shredded hats and shoes to give them added flare. Yet, she is crying. Again. And *he* is responsible.

It shall be my privilege and honor to ensure he pays for every illicit teardrop.

When I first met Miss Jane, I made a quality decision to accept her worship as my due. I even vowed to protect her with each of my nine lives. In a surprise twist even I myself did not see coming, I have decided to keep my word. Turns out, she... isn't terrible. I sometimes enjoy tolerating her even though she always melts at the sight of Conrad's annoying smile. And his equally annoying frown. Still, I'm willing to go to great lengths to facilitate her happiness.

My enemy's puny mind cannot even begin to fathom the lines I'm willing to cross to accomplish my goal. I'll make him rue the cold November morning he moved into my cottage and—oh, a bird!

# CHAPTER ONE

In *The Twelve Days of Christmas* song, everyone focuses on the partridge. I say concentrate on the pear...shaped diamond. What better way to break a curse than a holiday proposal?

–Lily Ladling's Holiday Advice for Ladies Cursed in Love

*The cold November morning*

"Conrad told me he loves me, and he's moving to Aurelian Hills." Jane Ladling knelt before the crackling hearth in her living room, going through a tattered box of fall decorations. She'd found the treasures in the old business center of her ancestral "estate," a landlocked cemetery named Garden of Memories. "The nerve of some people!"

Conrad Ryan. The Prince of Spices, thanks to his incredible scent, moving to her small town. For good. Being his ridiculously charming self. The horror!

"I assure you," she said primly, "I responded as calmly and

GENA SHOWALTER & JILL MONROE

rationally as possible and did the most logical thing. I broke up with him and got out of there fast." For a good reason!

Like all the women in her family, Jane was cursed. Fall in love with a guy and lose him. That wasn't the worst of it. If a breakup didn't take and a Ladling lady married the object of her affection, she all but signed his death certificate. Zero exceptions. A fact she hated even acknowledging.

None of her female relatives had ever beat their significant others to the grave. Grandma Lily lost Pops to a heart attack. Great grandmother Opal just straight up lost great grandfather Benjamin, who vanished one night, never to be heard from again. Opal did remarry years later, once Benjamin was pronounced dead, but the second husband died in a freak accident. And those were the tame stories in Jane's family tree.

For her, love equaled heartbreak. No, thank you. She had endured her fair share already. But...Here and now, she kinda sorta possibly, well...missed Conrad. So dang bad. They'd only dated for a few short weeks. Had only known each other a handful of months. But they'd been the best months and weeks of her life. During the thirteen endless days since their breakup, her internal pity party had never ceased.

"No comments or questions?" Jane asked her companion.

Rolex, her beloved fur-child, stretched across her grandmother's favorite afghan, staring at her from the back of the couch. No doubt the house panther's bored expression hid a well of concern for his agitated mother.

"I *had* to end things with him. I mean, what other choice did I have?" Jane demanded. "Conrad is too amazing. He deserves to live."

Silence. Not even a sympathetic meow.

Sighing, she reached inside the box, drew out a sign that read *Hello Fall*. Well, it was supposed to read Hello Fall. The

4

O had fallen off. She sat back on her haunches. Earlier, she'd decided to distract herself from the disaster of her life by decorating her home, the caretaker's cottage, for the first time since her Grandma Lily's death. A failed plan, obviously.

"Think about it. Conrad's hot enough to burn a woman's corneas. He's smart. Loyal. Strong. A bit stoic at times. Okay, a lot stoic *most* times." But Jane could make him laugh without trying. A talent she alone possessed, with an outcome she treasured. "And he's got the coolest job. Well, he used to have the coolest job." At the conclusion of his last case, the special agent had put in his notice at the Georgia Bureau of Homicide. Yesterday marked his final day. "He's a nearly extinct brand of people. Honest. Loyal."

Jane set the sign aside and withdrew another item, wrapped in old newspaper. A gentle unrolling revealed a ceramic pumpkin with the paint rubbed off one eye. How cute. A pumpkin pirate.

"But," she added. "The break-up was for the best. If ever I made the mistake of falling in love with him, he would propose marriage, we'd adopt a dozen fur-babies, and Conrad would die."

A little sadness now saved her from total destruction later. Growing to depend on Conrad, only to lose him, well, could anything be more terrible? Allowing *Rolex* to depend on him? A far worse crime. She owed both males her best due diligence. Hence the breakup. Besides, Conrad hadn't called or texted or begged her to reconsider. Not once. So he loved her? Ha! He'd abandoned her forever just because she'd told him never to contact her again. What a jerk!

"Now, that's quite enough about the world's tastiest man-candy," she said with a firm nod. "After I get these decorations unpacked, I'll treat myself to some homemade banana nut bread and open the early Christmas gift from Fiona."

Fiona Lawrence, a sixty-two-year-old grandmother, and one of the best people ever born. Jane's best friend.

Okay. She forced her attention to the box before her. The next item to gain its freedom was a leather-bound book of rustic brown, with a large L stamped into the lower right corner. Not a volume she'd encountered before. Intrigued, she untied the straps and skimmed the opening pages.

How wonderful. An old journal, handwritten by Benjamin Ladling. Opal's first husband and Pops's bio-dad. The one who'd disappeared without a trace a year after their wedding.

Why had her grandmother boxed up her father-in-law's journal with a bunch of fall decorations, rather than adding the tome to the Ladling library? So far, the passages offered only notes about daily operations at the cemetery—nope. Jane spoke too soon. The notes morphed into wild ramblings about a fleur-de-lys symbol and a hunt for hidden gold.

Goodness gracious! Gold again? Periodically rumors surfaced in town about an (alleged) cult known as the Order of Seven. The claims centered around a former gravekeeper—and founding member—who found a treasure trove of nuggets during Georgia's gold rush. Some townsfolk thought he'd stashed the wealth inside coffins just before their burials. Benjamin had clearly been a believer.

Jane read a few passages, her jaw growing slack. "He dug up plots and busted headstones during his search," she told Rolex. The irreverence!

A folded sheet of yellowed paper, once tucked between two of the pages, fluttered into her lap. Handling with care, she eased the ends apart. Hmm. A list of utter nonsense.

1. Mule easel
2. Barreling dads gin
3. Inhaled mist

4. Island is gall
5. Wailing milk
6. Bury handgun rod
7. Sunken ice naps

What the—*what?* This might be a mystery for Team Truth. A group consisting of Jane and her closest friends. Fiona and her boyfriend Sheriff Raymond Moore, who planned to retire in the next few months. Beauregard "Beau" Harden. Holden Bishop. Lucas "Trick" Robichaud. And Isaac Redding. Rolex acted as the official mascot, of course.

Jane looked over the notes Benjamin scribbled in the margins. Hmm. Looked like he'd experimented with different ciphers, attempting to decode the nonsense phrases on the list. He'd also been obsessed with circles. Wow. He'd drawn rings on every available space.

Ohhh. Benjamin had believed the list of seven was part of his treasure hunt, hadn't he? Did he think the phrases were keys to finding the gold?

Had he actually found gold—the very treasure some town's people believed remained hidden here? Curious, Jane flipped to the last passage he'd written. Well. It ended abruptly. In fact, he'd halted writing mid-sentence.

*I'm right. I know I'm right. I'd bet my life on it. I would even*

Gah! Why had he stopped there? She needed to know because…. just because! And there was a way to find out. All she had to do was retrace Benjamin's steps, going on a treasure hunt of her own. Bonus: She might gain a true distraction from her troubles and a boost to lift her out of her post-farewell-to-the-best-tush-in-the-GBH depression.

Something Jane had learned after finding three dead bodies on her property—she thrived during investigations.

A hard double rap sounded at her front door. With a gasp, she whipped up her head. Conrad! Only he knocked with such authority and distinction. Her heartbeat kicked into warp speed. Her ex was here. Why?

Rolex acted as Jane felt; he jumped to attention, his hair standing on end, his claws flaring.

She set the journal aside and scrambled to her feet. Tremors plagued her limbs as she smoothed the sides of her dress. Seriously, what was the former special agent doing here? Should she face him, or stay still and quiet until he bolted?

The hard double rap sounded again. "I know you're home, Jane. Let me in. We need to talk."

His husky voice sent shivers down her spine, and she moaned. Talk? Had he come to request another chance with her, after all?

Flutters erupted in her belly. Head high and palms damp, she marched to the entrance and twisted the knob. Hinges squeaked, her home opening up to the outside world...and there he stood. Tall, muscular and gorgeous, with dark hair, bronzed skin and a powerful body framed in fading sunlight.

He wore a cable-knit sweater and worn jeans, the hems frayed a bit around his combat boots. Heat radiated from him, chasing away the evening chill. The world's most incredible scent hit her awareness. Dry cedar and those tantalizing spices. *Will never get enough of his smell.*

A duffel bag dangled from one of his hands. A leash hung from the other, with an orange and white corgi named Cheddar panting at the end of it. The pooch used to belong to a nurse currently in prison awaiting trial for murder. At the woman's request, Conrad had taken over the pet's care. A kind, caring deed that made him even hotter. Not that Jane had noticed.

Rolex took a post at her feet, daring the adorable canine to come any closer.

"Hello, Jane." Conrad all but purred the words.

"Mr. Ryan," she replied, hoping the formal address masked her sudden breathlessness.

The corners of his mouth curved up. Nope. There'd been no masking. "Mr. Ryan," he said. "I like it. Makes me feel bossy."

Um, was he flirting with her? "You can't win me back," she blurted out to save his very life.

His amusement only intensified. "Who says I'll try?"

Ouch. So, yeah, that kind of stung. "Yes. Well. I'm doing magnificently, by the way. Some might even say glorious. Not that you asked. You look as if you're doing magnificently and glorious as well. Some might say *too* magnificent and glorious but that's neither here nor there." *Stop rambling!* "Anyway. How are *you*? Truly? How's life as a new fur-dad?"

"Fatherhood agrees with me. Cheddar is a very good boy." His gaze slid over Jane's purple fit and flare. "You look as lovely as usual."

See! Ridiculously charming. "Thank you." Needing protection from his incredible appeal, she crossed her arms over her middle. "Why are you here, Conrad?"

"Happy to explain." He leaned in and kissed her cheek. "Over drinks."

She blinked at him, her pulse racing. "Uh…"

A wide grin blooming, he stepped around her to lead the eager pup inside the cottage. Rolex, the world's most perfect feline, hissed and darted off. He'd met the corgi once before and hadn't scratched or bopped him a single time. Meaning, yes, they were basically best friends.

Heart thumping against her ribs, Jane pivoted and

followed Conrad deeper into the house. Into the kitchen, to be exact, where he puttered around as if he owned the place. And oh, he looked good doing it. As if he belonged among the chipped yellow laminate countertops and mushroom covered bread box and canister set. A favorite of Grandma Lily, who'd done the decoupage herself.

As the bane of Jane's existence poured two glasses of sweet tea, she eased into a barstool on the other side of the counter, next to her guest's bag. Cheddar settled at Conrad's feet, and Rolex jumped on the counter to glare at the dog. So precious!

"Why are you here?" Jane repeated softly. Being around him, knowing she couldn't lean against him and wouldn't feel him wrap his strong arms around her, was too painful.

"Someone sabotaged your car last month." He drained half the contents of his glass. "The culprit is still out there, and I plan to find them."

Oh yeah. Her car. The attempt to end her life. A mystery she preferred to forget. Who wanted to remember a near death experience? "I've already provided you with a formal statement and all the information at my disposal."

"And we'll be going over it again. Together. *After* we square away some personal business."

Her brow wrinkled even as her heart leaped. "*Personal business?*"

"That's right." His gaze held hers as he drained the rest of his glass. Dang it. Why was even that so sexy? "I'd like to rent your guest room while I'm looking for a place to stay here in town," he stated. "Before you say no, don't. Hear my offer first."

The moisture in her mouth dried. Conrad...living in her home... with her... maybe walking around after a shower with a towel cinched to his waist and water dripping from his hair...

Jane lost her breath. *Um, where was I headed with that line of thought?*

She swallowed, hard. "Go on. I'm listening." No! Bad! Not what she'd meant to say.

"While I'm here," he continued with a smooth tone, "I'll demonstrate how to run a proper investigation… and I'll pay attention when you explain how your way is better."

She opened her mouth to protest. But then the last part of his offer sank in. She *had* found three murderers, thank you, proving her way of solving crime was far superior to his. This was her chance to tell him all about it. Talk about an incomparable temptation! Especially since she intended to hunt for great grandfather Benjamin's gold. Conrad could help. Maybe. Sort of. But.

"We'll be roommates." Jane had never lived with a girl-friend, much less a former boyfriend. The thought of sharing her space…maybe kinda sorta wasn't the absolute worst.

"It'll only be for a few weeks. Possibly a few months." He refilled his glass with a rock steady hand. "I'll even help with chores."

Okay, so, that sounded amazingly wonderful. Too good. Her shoulders rolled in. "Why don't you stay in Atlanta?"

"I can't run for sheriff of Aurelian Hills and not live here. With a retiring sheriff and three murders in as many months, the town needs someone with my experience. Plus, there's no better place to raise my new fur-son."

Well. Darn. She couldn't argue with such bulletproof logic. There was no man more perfect for the job. And her hometown *was* an amazing place to raise fur-children, despite those murders. The rolling hills and lush trees couldn't be beat. The sense of community provided endless comfort.

"We might not be dating," he added, tilting his head and

11

peering at her through the thick shield of his lashes, "but we can still be friends. Right?"

Friends. With Conrad. It wasn't a horrendous idea. Though friends didn't daydream about kissing each other, they still enjoyed each other's company. Plus, it *would* be nice to learn the tricks of his trade. And to ensure he picked a good home. Also to inoculate herself against his rugged appeal. Seriously, how better to be un-charmed by someone than to live with them?

Was she reaching? She was reaching, wasn't she?

But... Rolex could use a friend, too. He'd been so depressed lately. Ever since he'd lost his girlfriend, Cartier. Long story. And that wasn't reaching; that was called being a good mom.

Super detective Conrad sensed her uncertainty and seized the opportunity to advance his cause. "Please Jane."

Ugh. The word *please* on those soft, sweet lips. *Look anywhere but at him.* Her gaze fell onto the leather-bound book that once belonged to her distant relative. "Okay, here's the deal. You can move in–" she began.

His eyes lit with triumph.

"–but I must warn you..."

"That you sleepwalk? Snore so loud you shake the walls? Bake cookies in the middle of the night? I'm hoping it's the last, by the way."

Jane chewed on the inside of her cheek. "I've recently come into possession of a very big clue that may lead to lost gold. You, of course, will help me find it in exchange for room and board. On top of everything else you've mentioned. And anything I think of later."

A groan chased away his previous triumph. "Are we talking about the gold that has caused so much trouble for you already, bringing treasure hunters and their shovels out of the shadowy underground of Aurelian Hills? The very gold that has made three corpses out of perfectly alive people?"

She nodded. "We are."

He scrubbed a hand down his face. "The very gold that, if found, will draw more and more people to your land? People who are willing to do anything to strike it rich?"

"Yes, of course. Conrad, I'm not seeing your point." Her breath came out as a restless sigh. "So? What's your answer? Are we officially roomies or not?"

# CHAPTER TWO

You know what's interesting about turtle doves? There are two of them. They are partners in song. Forever.

–Lily Ladling's Holiday Advice for Ladies Cursed in Love

*M*oaning, Jane stretched atop her bed and blinked open her eyes. She'd tossed and turned for hours after researching the list of nonsensical phrases and making no real progress. Now, she was wide awake at–she rolled over to glance at her clock–three in the morning. Yikes. Sleeping across the hall from her favorite ex was going to suck, wasn't it? Especially because Conrad truly preferred friendship to a relationship.

*We might not be dating, but we can still be friends, right?*

His words rang inside her mind. So her stomach knotted because of them. So what? His happiness and well-being mattered more than her desire to–nothing. Bottom line: They *were* friends, no matter what. But did he have to be so upbeat after the collapse of their once-in-a-lifetime romance?

Well, if he could be cheery and bright, she could too. The perfect mood for opening Fiona's gift. *Oh! That's right.* Conrad's unexpected arrival had completely distracted Jane from the present.

She snapped on the bedside light. Rolex perched on the pillow beside hers. He stared at her, hard, as if trying to see into her soul, and it was the cutest thing in the world.

"Such a good boy." She scratched him behind the ears before reaching for the wooden box tied with a bright yellow ribbon. With trembling hands, she lifted the lid. The familiar scent of Pops's favorite cigar tickled her nose. Her eyelids turned heavy and sank low as she let cherished memories wash over her. The puzzles she and her grandfather used to work together. The mystery stories he'd read to her. How he'd held her hand whenever he'd presided over a funeral.

A soft smile grew as she refocused on the journal. Spying a familiar flowing handwriting on twelve envelopes nestled inside the box, she gasped. Grandma Lily's beloved script! Jane read to Rolex. "Lily Ladling's Holiday Advice for Ladies Cursed in Love." Aw. How precious!

A thirteenth envelope bore Fiona's distinct no-nonsense scrawl–*Open First.*

With great enthusiasm, Jane slid a finger beneath the flap and quickly tugged a single sheet of paper from the envelope.

*Dear Jane,*
*Your grandma and I had a pact. If I died before her, she*
*would make sure my son never acts the fool and leaves his*
*wife. In return, I was to make sure you received these letters*
*of advice from Lily at Christmas... after you fell in love. I*
*believe that time is now. Your grandma loved you more*
*than a basket of Georgia peaches on the hottest summer*

*day, hon. She wanted you to be happy. I hope you listen to her.*
*I cherish you as if you are my own,*

*Fiona*

*PS: This bit of wisdom is from me: Want to change your fate? Change your thoughts.*

Drawing in a shuddering breath, Jane held the dear box of letters to her chest. Warmth and pure love hugged her in return. A flood of emotion left her shaky but elated. How like her darling grandmother to look after her from the grave.

Jane reached for the first letter. Tears burned her eyes, and her throat tightened as she read...

*My sweet Jane. In the Twelve Days of Christmas song, everyone focuses on the partridge. I say concentrate on the pear...shaped diamond. The holiday is a wonderful time for a proposal.*

Jane's shoulders began to shake, the pressure in her throat easing. A smile broke free. *Only my grandmother.*

With the advice playing through her mind, any remaining tension deserted her. Peace reigned. She returned the letters to the box and retied the ribbon. Hey! Rolex was still staring at her.

After blowing him a kiss, she flicked off her light, hoisted up her covers and snuggled into her pillow. Finally sleep came...

*BANG. Clink. Clang.*

Jane jolted upright. Panting, she scanned her bedroom. What in the heck was that awful noise?

Morning sunlight streamed through a crack in her light purple curtains, illuminating a slightly cluttered bedroom. Not that the collection of hats counted as part of the clutter. Or the stack of clothes in the chair by the closet. Nothing out of the ordinary caught her notice. What— memories came flooding back, and her jaw slackened. Breakup. Journal. Gold. Conrad. Car. Gift. *Roommates.*

With far more energy than Jane expected, she bounced out of bed. "Come on, Rolex. Let's—" Um, where was Rolex? Already out and about in the cottage, on guard duty?

She brushed her teeth in her private bathroom, then secured a pink terry cloth robe over her flannel pajamas and set out to find her cat. If she happened to run into Conrad in the process, well, that couldn't be helped. Wait. Was that…it was! She frowned and picked up a hat in the middle of her floor, murdered by cat claws.

Well. Rolex must have mistaken the item for a toy. Silly boy.

Downstairs she went, her belly fluttering. Conrad, Cheddar and Rolex occupied the kitchen. Conrad stood before the stove, flipping pieces of frying bacon in a skillet. The meat sizzled, but so did he. Locks of his thick dark hair were askew. He wore a white T-shirt and dark blue sweatpants. Tattoos decorated both of his arms. Each image looked like something drawn by a child. Stick figures. Unidentifiable animals. A smiling sun, a colorful rainbow, and a puffy cloud.

His biceps flexed with his movements, and Jane fanned her overheating cheeks.

Cheddar sat near his new dad, no doubt praying a bit of bacon fell to the floor. Rolex perched in the centerpiece bowl on the kitchen table, watching their guests with a thousand ideas seeming to churn behind his unwavering glare.

"Good morning, Jane," Conrad said, tossing her a smile over his shoulder. "My apologies for the racket."

Dang it. She missed the days he'd called her "sweetheart."

"Hungry?" he asked.

Her pulse leaped, and she ran her bottom lip between her teeth. "Ravenous," she whispered. Gah! *Get it together, Jay Bird.* "Uh. I mean, yes. A little." She scratched both animals behind the ears before settling in at the counter.

"By the way, I have a contact who was able to dig up an old town newspaper article about your great grandfather's disappearance." Conrad cracked a couple eggs into the same pan as the bacon. "There's not much detail in it. The most interesting part is a quote from your great grandmother."

Instantly intrigued, Jane leaned over the counter and made grabby hands at him. "Tell me faster!"

He tossed another smile over his shoulder. "I like you eager." As she reeled over the innocently suggestive statement, he returned his attention to the food and continued, never missing a beat. "She said her husband woke her up in the middle of the night excited about something in the mausoleum. He dressed and hurried off, and she went back to sleep. He never returned."

"The mausoleum? I'll return in a jiff." She jumped to her feet and raced to the back of the cottage. Benjamin's journal rested on the old desk, right at home amongst the archives of a cemetery dating back centuries. A swift grab, and she was on her way to the kitchen. On the stool once more, she told Conrad between panting breaths, "I remember seeing a passage about the mausoleum."

While she attempted to skim the pages to find the reference, he finished cooking breakfast, made her a plate and claimed the seat beside her. Not concentrating on him fully proved difficult. He just…he looked so casual. So at home. So perfect.

Why, why, why did the breakup have to be for the greater good?

"As for our other case," he said after swallowing a bite of eggs. "I've got Beau looking into security feed from businesses near the places you parked the day of your car accident. And that's Professor Ryan's first lesson in Investigation 101. Never hesitate to delegate a task to a trusted source with a better skillset."

Ohhhh. Professor Ryan. *You get an A for effort.* "Delegate, meaning to allow someone else to horn in on my investigation? No, thank you. And that is the first lesson in my class, The Right Way." She glanced up from the journal. "Well?"

He arched a brow, his amber irises sparkling. "Well what?"

"Aren't you going to write down my pearl of wisdom? My class has pop quizzes and semester tests."

Now he snorted. Tweaking the tip of her nose, he said, "Brat." Exactly what he used to do when they'd dated.

Her chest clenched with longing. Moving on. "I'm not sure I'll ever believe someone hated me enough to rig my hearse to blow carbon monoxide in my face." A horror now known as "the Incident." She'd passed out, crashed, and woken up in an ambulance.

Voice like granite, Conrad told her, "I'm certain I won't stop until I find the one responsible."

A dreamy sigh threatened to escape. *Focus on the journal.* Right. Jane skimmed the pages until…yes! "Here." The folded note with the list of nonsense. She explained the phrases as she spread the ends and tapped the mention. "Benjamin circled and underlined the words *mausoleum* and *map* with three question marks beside each."

"You want to check out the mausoleum after we eat?" Conrad asked.

Not before? Fine. "A thousand percent I do." Jane shoveled bites into her mouth, one after the other. Scrambled eggs, crisp bacon and buttery toast. Not bad. In fact, kind of delicious.

*And he's a breakfast aficionado too?* How was that even fair to womankind? If he mastered the fine art of blueberry pancakes, the greatest food known to mankind, she would have no choice but to beg *him* for another chance.

As if reading her mind, he said, "None of my famous cinnamon sugar french toast for you. You aren't ready."

"What are you even talking about? I'm always ready for french toast!" Wait. Not always. "I mean, of course, I'll accept french toast if blueberry pancakes aren't an option."

"Either way, you aren't ready for these. My specialty. I'm told they are world changing."

Whoa, whoa, whoa. Someone else had sampled his cinnamon sugar french toast? Who? When? Where? Jane swallowed a whimper of desperate curiosity and finished cleaning her plate. Better to focus on the gold mystery.

The second she swallowed the last bite, she clasped Conrad's hand. He'd only eaten half of his portion, but he didn't protest when she drew him to his feet.

"Come on," she rushed out. "You need shoes."

He was in the process of tearing into his toast as she nudged him toward the stairs. Rather than protest, he devoured the bread as he climbed, Cheddar following him. Less than a minute later, her new roommate was clomping down in his combat boots, sans dog, wearing a sweatshirt over his T-shirt.

Jane rushed to the entryway closet, where she donned her coat, a stocking cap with cat ears, and the rubber boots she kept downstairs for emergencies such as this. "Cheddar isn't coming?"

"He jumped on the bed and fell asleep before I finished tying the first shoelace. I didn't have the heart to wake him."

She led Conrad outside, calling, "Rolex, honey, I expect to find Cheddar in the same condition I'm leaving him. Love you. Okay bye!" Warmth gave way to a pine-scented chill as the door closed behind them.

As Jane and Conrad walked the cobblestone path side by side, muted sunlight bathed the gentle rolling hills to the right and the various angel statues before her. She almost clasped his hand ten thousand times.

To fill the silence and distract herself, she asked, "Are you looking to rent or buy?"

"Buy. Being a property owner will only help my cause."

He wasn't wrong. "Have you chosen a real estate agent yet?"

His amber eyes sparkled again. He was about to tease her, wasn't he? "According to the Headliner, Abigail Waynes-Kirkland just got her real estate license." The Headliner was a town message board and weekly paper.

"You absolutely cannot work with a gravedigger, Conrad." Too far, too far! "I forbid it."

"Noted," he said with a grin.

Abigail, her brother, and her ex-husband were treasure hunters who'd come to the cemetery with a shovel, hoping to unearth those rumored nuggets. "You should ask Fiona to help you. Her husband sold homes before their divorce, so she's practically an expert."

"Actually, I already have a realtor. Buddy Horn of Horn Realty." He nudged her shoulder with his own and offered a grin. The adorable lopsided one that made her knees quiver. Her favorite. "You got any beef with him?"

"No. I don't think I have." But anyone was better than Abigail Waynes-Kirkland.

They traveled through Eden Valley, over the bridge into Autumn Grove, past the headstone belonging to Muffin, the cemetery's first and only canine resident, and to the Greek-revival style vestibule mausoleum of blue-gray granite. Impressive columns stretched from the portico floor. As a little girl, she would stare at the gabled roof topped with a swan's neck finial.

Jane pushed open the massive bronze doors, which time and the Georgia weather had gentled and turned virescent. Their footsteps echoed amongst the masonry and high ceilings. They paused by a small area of low benches in an open, triangular design for visitors to reflect or pray. She often found a single flower in full bloom left on the floor during her daily rounds.

"Tell me about the mural," Conrad said, motioning to the panorama landscape etched into the stone walls. His arm fell to his side, his fingers brushing hers, and she forgot to breathe for a moment.

"It's, um, a map of the grounds." She motioned to different landmarks, doing her best to hide her sudden trembling and fighting the urge to lean her head upon his shoulder. "See?" she said, pointing. "The original business center. Pleasant Green. Serenity Rose. Paradise Ladling." Where Grandma Lily, Pops, and Opal were buried, along with a dozen ancestors she'd never met. "Since it's out of the elements, it stays pretty much the same. From time to time, we bring in someone to touch it up."

She studied the images as Conrad strode through the surprisingly wide space. The list of seven churned through her mind. "When you hear 'sunken ice naps,' what's the first thing that comes to your mind?"

"Something buried in water?" he suggested, then twisted his lips. "That might be too obvious."

"Could it have something to do with diamonds?" she wondered aloud, following his path. "Say...diamonds buried with the dead?"

"It's possible." He turned slowly. Only then did she realize how close she stood to him. He must have realized it, too. Eyes darkening, he reached out and tucked a strand of hair behind her ear. "But which dead?"

She gulped. "Um. Exactly." And how did 'mule easel' fit into anything? She scanned the map. Her shoulder brushed Conrad's, and they both stilled. Her breath hitched. She hurried to the shadows, putting distance between them. "There's no, um, X marks the spot that I can see."

"Of course not. That would be too easy."

Silence stretched as she forced her mind to focus on the matter at hand. "Do you get anything for the phrase inhaled mist? Island is gall? Wailing milk?"

"Let me think for a second."

"I see Operation Infiltrate is a go," someone else announced.

The familiar voice registered. Conrad turned as Jane exited the dark alcove. Beau, another dear friend she cherished, towered in the mausoleum's open doorway. A blond beefcake with a craggily outer shell and a soft, gooey center.

"Hey, Beau." Jane and Beau had met as children. He'd moved away a few years later, then returned to town as a smoking hot war vet who owned Peach State Security, the company overseeing the Garden's safety. He must be doing his morning rounds. She smiled and waved.

"Jane," he said, lifting his sunglasses, revealing piercing green eyes. "I didn't see you there."

"What's Operation Infiltrate?" And why was she just now

hearing about it? She preferred to be on the ground floor of every mission, whatever that mission happened to be.

"My move to town and bid for sheriff." Conrad strode over and plucked the sunglasses from the other man's grip, then fit the shades on his own face. "What else?"

"Right," Beau said. "What else?"

They were almost as cute as Rolex and Cheddar. And dang. Bromances must be in the air. When would it be girl-friend season?

"Find anything in the security footage?" Conrad asked the other man.

Beau shook his head. "I didn't. Jane parked in a blind spot for about half an hour. However, here's the name of a deputy and the woman he ticketed." He handed over a folded sheet of paper. "They were parked nearby for fourteen of those thirty minutes. Maybe one of them saw something without realizing they saw something."

Oh! A promising lead. "Why don't you two go on?" Jane shooed them both outside before joining them. Standing between them, she shut the mausoleum door. "I'm going to do my own morning rounds and study Benjamin's journal." Let the boys handle the vehicular sabotage without her today.

Being Conrad's friend was a bit tougher than she'd imagined. She could use a break from him. Besides, she didn't need to hear townspeople speculate about all the reasons someone might wish to harm her.

"Who's Benjamin?" Beau asked.

"She'll explain later." Her new roommate stepped in front of her, blocking her path. The dark lenses hid whatever emotion glimmered in his eyes, but the compression of his lips said plenty. Something had irritated him. "How can you learn my investigative methods—or tell me what I'm doing wrong—if we aren't together?"

Ah. Okay. She understood his attitude now. Conrad Ryan possessed pride in spades, and he balked at the thought of not paying the agreed upon fee for his room and board. "Fine. I'll go to town and tag team witnesses with you and Beau." The vet could serve as a friendship chaperone. "But. From now on, you've got to include me in all things Operation Infiltrate. I have skills you know nothing about. I add value to any team, I promise."

He unveiled a slow, devastating grin. "Deal. Except Beau is busy, so he's staying here."

"Busy," Beau echoed. "So much stuff to do."

What? They'd be going alone? Just Jane and Conrad?

Forget car accidents, gold hunters, and murder times three. She feared her heart might not survive this.

# CHAPTER THREE

French hens are tasty birds. Do you know what else is tasty?
Romance. Served on a platter of love and sprinkled with
trust and loyalty.

–Lily Ladling's Holiday Advice for Ladies Cursed in Love

*C*onrad's beast of a car roared to life with the push of a
button. Used to his boring Georgia Bureau of Homicide standard issue sedan, Jane had almost lost her footing after
spotting the sleek, black roadster parked in front of her cottage.
The vehicle looked like nothing she'd ever seen before: raw,
powerful and utterly unique. He'd once mentioned how he
enjoyed restoring old cars. He'd even rebuilt the hearse after
the Incident. Had he pieced this beauty together all on his own?

She shouldn't ask. The less she knew about him the
better. Except...

"Did you build this car?" She had to know.

He fiddled with the screen on his dash. "Stella is more than a car."

Ahh, so Jane had another woman to compete with for his attention. *Wait. Nope. You're single. He's single. Stella wins this game.* "Tell me about her."

He obliged. Oh, did he oblige. He spent the entire ride into town talking about direct fuel injection and increasing downforce. His enthusiasm was infectious. She caught herself smiling and asking questions about aerodynamics even though she knew nothing about the subject. When it came to cars, the only thing she cared about was whether it had gas. But dang it, did he have to speak of the other woman in his life so enthusiastically?

He parked in an empty spot across from the law offices of Hagger, Hagger and Miller. Near the spot she'd parked before her accident. Devin Hagger, the only partner remaining at the firm, was the most prestigious lawyer in town. Hagger had once been in business with Tony Miller, the man murdered at the Garden during a party thrown by Jane. Hagger had also been a top suspect—to Jane.

"Come on. I'll show you my process," Conrad said. They emerged into the cold morning. And, for the next half hour, they stood at the side of the road. Silent. After the shoulder bump and finger graze in the mausoleum, she purposely remained ten paces away from him.

Conrad stared here, there and everywhere, the wheels in his head obviously churning.

"What are we doing again?" Jane asked, drawing the lapels of her cashmere fleece tighter. A garment she cherished, and a gift made by Grandma Lily simply because Jane had liked the striking yarn the color of wild berries.

"We're seeing what Adaline Crema saw before we speak with her." He pulled a notebook from his pocket and wrote something down. "She's the one who was ticketed the day of your accident."

Jane remembered that day well, and not just because of the wreck. Earlier, Hagger had told her, *"Your snooping is gonna get you into trouble. You keep at it, and you may not like what you find. Or who finds you."*

A promise–or an accurate prediction? Had she poked her nose into the wrong person's business?

A shudder wracked her, despite the warmth provided by her beloved coat. *Concentrate on the now.*

"Detective work is boring," Jane grumbled. She much preferred her version of fact-finding–searching through a dead woman's purse or barreling through a suspect's place of business.

Though, really, Conrad's brand of investigation did provide stimulating visuals. A beam of golden sunlight spotlighted the soon-to-be sheriff–no way he'd lose the election–as if drawn to him like a magnet. She knew the feeling. Did he have to look so gorgeous? Before they'd left the cottage, he'd changed into his usual perfectly tailored suit and tie, paired with an extremely sexy wool coat.

The cold breeze carried hints of his scent. Prince of Spices indeed. She closed her eyes for a moment, just a moment, and breathed deep. A mistake. Awareness for him zinged her every cell, her response to him undeniable and inescapable.

He crooked his finger at her. With a voice of pure temptation, he invited, "Come here, Jane."

Ugh. Close contact still wasn't a good idea. But. Business was business, right? Dragging her feet, she made her way over. The second she stepped within range, he reached out, clasped her hand, and tugged her in front of him. Then he released her—but only to grip her waist to hold her steady. Shivers rolled over her spine.

With his lips hovering over her ear, he softly commanded, "Tell me what you see." His warmth made a mockery of her coat.

More shivers plagued her, each one hot enough to spark a new wildfire in her veins. *Red alert! Red alert!* She scrambled for another source of focus. "Townsfolk bustling down the sidewalk. Pots displaying colorful mums of orange and yellow outside storefronts."

"Good," he said. "Now imagine you are Ms. Crema, and you are parked here. The hearse is there." Again he released her, but only long enough to point to the spot she'd parked the day of her crash. "What can you deduce?"

The urge to melt into him bombarded her. *Only friends, remember?* "Um. Well. Our person of interest had a view of the passenger side of my vehicle. She could have seen anyone approaching from the...north?"

"South."

"Yes. That." So directions outside of the Garden weren't her thing. So what? "But Ms. Crema wouldn't have noticed anyone coming from the alleyway behind all those shops."

"True."

So... "Conrad, I don't mean to insult you, but I deduced this information with a single glance, yet you required over thirty minutes."

A soft chuckle left him, his breath fanning over her hair. "I've run about fifty different scenarios through my head."

Ahhh. Okay. Yes. That made sense. Why hadn't she thought of it? "My turn to run scenarios." Let's see, let's see. "Oh! How about this? The deputy who pulled her over was the one messing with my car. When he finished up with his dastardly plot to end my life, he climbed into his cruiser and noticed the indomitable Adaline toddling past. Afraid she saw something she shouldn't, he hurried to pull her over and cover his tracks. He questioned her subtly but learned nothing. Next he did the only thing he could. Issued her a ticket—and a threat." In her best evil overlord imitation, she said, "Tell anyone what you saw here today, and the next fine will cost double."

Conrad snorted. "What's the deputy's motive?"

Easy. "To possess Garden of Memories and get to the gold."

"Not bad. But I'd bet he did it because he has a secret crush on you."

As if. But she could play along. "Yes, and when he heard I was dating a certain GBH agent, he decided to punish me for betraying him—wait, you probably need a little backstory first. For the past seven years, the deputy and I have been married with three children. But only in his head. If he couldn't have me, no one could. Now that you and I are broken up, he's happy again. The reason there have been no other attempts to kill me."

A pause. Then, "The way your mind works." Fascination saturated his tone. "When Hollywood makes a movie about your life, it's going to be an instant blockbuster, I guarantee it."

Jane fluffed her hair. "A new, up and coming star will play me, no doubt, and Henry Cavill will portray you. Of course, you'll have to teach him how to do your patented convince-me-you're-not-guilty stare."

"Please," Conrad said with mock haughtiness. "You're either born with it or you're not."

A laugh escaped her. Dang, she liked this guy.

With a voice that reminded her of smoke wafting over gravel, he stated, "There's only one question remaining. Is this movie a crime drama or a romance?"

"Why can't it be both?" Eek! They were flirting, and it must stop. Soon. Within the next five or twenty minutes surely. No! Bad! It had to stop now, now, now. "So," she said, stepping away from him and losing his warmth. Instantly regretting it. "Since we're prepared to interrogate Ms. Crema, we should probably, well, interrogate Ms. Crema. By the way, I've never met her but I've heard of her. She supposedly eats nails for breakfast and glass shards for dessert."

He didn't miss a beat. "I've changed my mind. I'd rather speak with the deputy with the crush first."

The quick burst of a siren preceded a flash of blue and red lights, breaking their playful mood. Jane jumped, startled. A black and white patrol car eased up beside them. "I think you're gonna get your chance to talk to him sooner than expected," she said.

The window rolled down and a deputy leaned out the window, his reflective glasses glinting in the winter sunlight. Jane recognized him and knew he was the one Conrad sought! This street must be his "beat." That was the saying, wasn't it? Anyway. The guy wasn't someone Jane knew well, just someone she'd seen around. He was in his mid-forties, with graying hair and a pretty impressive beard.

"Do you know why I stopped you?" he asked, as if he'd just pulled them over for speeding.

If he wanted her to guess, she'd guess. Had her scenario been correct? Had the secret gold hunter returned to the scene of his crime? She opened her mouth to ask outright–the Jane Ladling way–but Conrad halted her by snaking his arm around her waist and giving her a squeeze. Right. Don't give the po-po anything.

"Why don't you tell us," Conrad said. A statement, not a question.

Lines crossed the deputy's forehead, and his lips turned down in a frown. Jane immediately understood his dilemma. The former special agent could become the other man's boss in a matter of months. Best to tread lightly. "Got a complaint about a couple loitering in the area, looking into car

31

windows and pulling on handles. We've had some trouble along the street recently."

Her spine stiffened. "Yes, and I was the beneficiary of that trouble."

The deputy glanced at Conrad before lifting his hands in surrender. "Just following up on a complaint, ma'am."

"Actually, I planned to stop by the station to discuss Ms. Ladling's wreck," Conrad said, "and the ticket you issued to Adaline Crema that day."

While Conrad handled the Q and A, Jane scanned the area. Who in the world had called in a complaint about them? A complaint filled with lies, no less. She eyed the shop windows but didn't notice anything out of the ordinary. Then her gaze lifted to a floor to ceiling window. Staring down at her was the short, stocky Devin Hagger. Him. He'd done it.

They were too far away for her to make out his expression, but she knew. Oh, she knew. He didn't like her, and he was just that petty.

But was he petty enough to sabotage her vehicle?

"Ready?" Conrad asked, stuffing his hands in his pockets as the deputy drove off. He ushered her to his car–er Stella— without touching her.

Their earlier ease had been completely eradicated. "Learn anything?"

"Not yet, but I'll be speaking with him again."

Once they were buckled in, Jane breathed in his scent once again. Before she could slip into another Conrad-haze, she opened Benjamin's journal and muttered, "Gonna read. No talkie-talkie."

She'd brought the book as a buffer. A way to forget they sat alone in a small space. And it worked. For several minutes, she lost herself in the drama of Benjamin's hunt for gold.

Then a sentence shocked a gasp out of her. She read it again. Then again. Nope, the words didn't change. "I think my great grandfather Benjamin had an affair." Furious on Opal's behalf, Jane read the words out loud. "Do I stay with my pregnant wife or leave with my darling Elise, who is also pregnant?" She fumed. "How could he?"

Conrad winced. "Yeah. That's pretty bad. To be fair, though, he doesn't say Elise's baby is his."

Still! Jane had fond memories of Opal returning to the Garden every summer before passing at the age of ninety-nine. The small, gray-haired woman had made the world's best homemade biscuits and sausage gravy. She used to rock Jane to sleep while staring out the window, as if waiting and watching for Benjamin to return home. Honestly, there'd been no sweeter or kinder woman. But of course, the Ladling curse overlooked no one. Had Benjamin run off with his precious Elise?

Or had he run off on his own, leaving both women behind? A cheater cheated.

A wave of sadness washed over Jane. And more anger. If Elise had lived in Aurelian Hills, she was most likely buried at the Garden. There'd been plenty of open plots back then and no other cemetery. Among the residents, two bore the name Elise. Elise Dansing and Mary Elise Sullivan.

Yes, Jane had memorized the guest list long ago. Anyway. Only one of the Elises had lived in the days of Benjamin and Opal. Elise Dansing, wife of Dr. Gabriel Dansing.

What was it with doctors and their six degrees away from scandal in this town?

Jane gulped. Dansing just happened to be the maiden name of Tiffany Hotchkins, a woman she'd accused of murder on three separate occasions. They weren't mortal enemies, but they weren't friends either.

Tiffany came from old money. Ancestors who'd struck it

rich in the gold mines. What if Benjamin had decided to run away with Elise the night he'd found his own supply of gold—if he'd found the gold, of course—but Elise had entertained other ideas? She could've killed Benjamin and stolen his newfound fortune, keeping every dime for herself.

"I probably shouldn't ask, but I'm a brave boy, so why not?" Conrad asked. "What's going on in that mind of yours?"

"I think Benjamin had an affair with—" Jane scrunched up her nose—"Tiffany Hotckkins's great grandmother."

"Let me guess. You're hoping to hunt down Tiffany for a chat before we do anything else?"

Jane ignored his wry tone and nodded. "Yes, please and thank you. Besides, she and Abigail were in town the day of my accident. I remember seeing them. So, who knows? Maybe I'll solve both cases with the first swing."

Turned out, Tiffany was indeed home this fine morning. According to sources at the Headliner, the rich widow never rose from bed before noon.

At 9:32, Conrad and Jane punched in the neighborhood's gate code that everyone in town learned within minutes of a change, thanks to the app, and parked in the Hotchkins's driveway. The sprawling, three-story mansion dazzled with its perfectly manicured yard and historic white columns.

In the good old dating days, Conrad would get out of a vehicle and rush to Jane's side to help her emerge. Today, she didn't give him a chance to sink into former boyfriend habits. If he reverted to such gentlemanly behavior, she'd melt into him; she knew she would. If he didn't, she might spend the rest of the day missing it. What? A girl should always know her weaknesses and faults.

Anyway. Jane set Benjamin's journal aside and entered the cold seconds behind Conrad. She smoothed the fabric of her yellow dress and covertly examined his expression. He still wore Beau's sunglasses, hiding whatever emotion glimmered in his amber eyes. What's more, his soft lips gave nothing away. Super soft. Beyond soft. But also firm the times they'd pressed against—Gah! *Not going there.*

Swallowing the lump in her throat, she kept pace at his side as they made their way to the porch, *not* holding hands. How her palm ached to anchor to his.

"You know what you want to ask her?" he asked, his fist hovering over the closed door. "You'll get only one answer out of her before she shuts the door in our faces, guaranteed."

A good guess, considering the animosity Tiffany bore towards her. Besides accusing the widow of murder thrice, Jane had proved her ex-fiancé guilty of murder. Which was really a favor, if you thought about it. But, okay, yes, she'd also ruined Tiffany's Halloween party by trapping a killer in her master bedroom.

"I don't mean to brag, Conrad, but I'm about to rock this." Probably. Mostly.

He snickered before he knocked his patented double rap. Then he knocked again. And again. He didn't stop until the door swung open, revealing Tiffany.

Her dark hair hung about her shoulders, messy but somehow delightful. She blinked against the morning sun, tightening the belt of a champagne-colored satin robe with lace circling the cuffs and hem, giving off an old Hollywood glam vibe. Did this woman never look bad? She'd just been disturbed mid-slumber, and there weren't even sheet creases on her cheeks.

"You." Tiffany narrowed her eyes. Her attention darted to

Conrad, and she scowled. "No. Nope. I'm not doing this again. I don't care who died this time. I didn't do it, and I'm not answering any—"

"No one died," Jane interjected. "But this *is* a matter of life and death." Truth. Benjamin had lived and died. Well, probably died. Though he received a funeral, his body was never found.

The widow flicked her tongue over an incisor. "Fine. I'll answer one question."

Of course, Conrad couldn't contain his smirk.

Jane lifted her chin. "What can you tell me about your great grandmother Elise?"

Tiffany's brow furrowed with confusion. "All I know is that my dad only ever referred to her as the old battle-ax. But what does she have to do with anything?"

Battle-ax? "Did she happen to disappear at some point in your family history?"

"No. Why?"

So the couple hadn't run off together. "Is she the Dansing ancestor who found gold? That's how your family made their money, right?"

"Gold?" Something glinted in Tiffany's eyes. "What are you trying to say, Jane?"

Nothing. Everything "I'm on an information hunt, that's all," she said. Because it was the heart of the truth.

Tiffany looked between Jane and Conrad a second time, her posture growing stiffer and stiffer. "Unless one of you explains what's going on, this conversation is over."

Conrad motioned to Jane. "Go ahead. You're rocking this."

She was, wasn't she? She'd already gotten three responses. "So. Yeah. There's a slight, almost not even worth mentioning chance that our great grandparents had an affair. There was a baby, you see, and–"

"What!" Tiffany shrieked. "Are you trying to tell me I have a long lost relative or–" The widow sucked in a breath. "You think we're related."

*Excuse me?* "No. Not in the least." Uh. Unless they *were* related? Dang. It was a possibility Jane hadn't considered. Technically, though, it was maybe, kind of, well, possible. Depending on the timing and all. "I don't actually know," she admitted. "But we can find out. If you would be kind enough to tell me—"

"No!" the other woman bellowed. "Absolutely not. I am not looking into this, and neither are you. We are dropping the matter here and now and never speaking of it again. And don't you dare try to claim my family fortune belongs to you." With that, the pale, distressed Tiffany slammed the door in Jane's face.

Well. "I gotta say. That went better than expected."

"That it did," Conrad stated, reaching for her hand. He stopped himself just before contact. A wry smile flashed, there and gone. He gestured toward the car. "Now you want to go home and dig into your family's past, yes?"

She didn't try to deny it. "Do you mind?"

"Not at all." Far from upset, he opened the passenger side door for her. "I'll drop you off. There are a few more people I plan to question. I'll bring Daisy's home for dinner and tell you everything I learn."

She adored Daisy's. Best food in town. But. "I'll cook." Jane did not need to be reminded of their first date, when they'd picnicked at his favorite childhood park and devoured the perfect meal from the five-star diner.

"Deal."

It was only later, as Jane searched the Ladling library in her office for other family journals that the truth hit her. Dinner. With Conrad. Just the two of them. Even without food from Daisy, the meal would feel like a date. And that, she couldn't allow.

Determined, she whipped out her phone and called Fiona.

"Two questions," she said as soon as her best friend answered. "Can you come over and how soon can you get here?"

# CHAPTER FOUR

We can learn a lot from calling birds. They keep their lines of communication open. That's probably the reason they stay together.

–Lily Ladling's Holiday Advice for Ladies Cursed in Love

*S*itting before the crackling hearth, sipping hot cocoa and breathing in the crisp scent of burning wood, Jane knitted with Fiona. Always a balm to her soul. Especially when Rolex cuddled up in her lap. For six years, she and her precious friend had met at least once a week to craft toys for children in need. Barring unforeseen circumstances, of course.

This time, however, Conrad reclined on the couch with Cheddar at his feet, reading *Law and Ordinance of Aurelian Hills*. A copy he'd borrowed from the Yellow Brick Abode Library, the only library in town. He'd already gotten a card!

His move to town was truly happening. And why in the world was Rolex staring at her so intently?

Aw. He was probably considering all the reasons he loved her.

"I adore you, too, baby," she told him.

"Lucky cat," Conrad muttered.

Wait. What? Jane's gaze zoomed back to her roommate. Surely she'd misheard him. Her knitting needle missed its mark, the tip stabbing her finger. Ow! She sucked in a breath. Rolex startled, jumping down. The darling feline used the opportunity to pounce on Cheddar. After a quick bop to the dog's nose, the housepanther darted off. What a playful, perfect boy. But seriously, what had Conrad meant by *lucky cat?*

He hadn't spoken much since his return from town, and she hadn't asked how things had gone. Yet. She didn't want to worry Fiona with talk of the Incident. The dear woman had enough fodder for stress on her plate 'o life, considering her boyfriend, Sheriff Raymond Moore, recently suffered a heart attack. The reason for his retirement and Conrad's plan to take over his job.

Although, since both Fiona and the sheriff had passed the sixty year mark a while back, the term "boyfriend" struck Jane as wrong. Manfriend? Romantic partner in crime solving?

Oh, to be one of the curse-less and fancy free.

Her gaze returned to the rumpled and relaxed Conrad. The gorgeous man hadn't batted an eye when Fiona arrived. He'd hugged the precious woman like a long, lost grandmother and mentioned his hunt for a place to live. Of course, despite his mysterious "lucky cat" comment, he'd walked away from Jane as easily as he'd walked away from his past relationships. Why care about keeping her all to himself?

*I deserve this, I really do.* As often as she'd attempted to cut

Conrad from her life, he deserved a chance to cut Jane from his. Her just desserts. But honestly, did he have to look so good while serving her tit for tat? He'd exchanged the suit for a bicep hugging T-shirt and worn jeans. Talk about a delicious slice of–

"Hello, hello, hello," Fiona prompted, waving her hand in front of Jane's face. "Five minutes ago, you asked me what I know about Opal and Benjamin. I'm guessing you'd like to hear the answer at some point tonight."

Eek! Caught ogling her roommate! "Yes. Right. So? What do you know?" Fiona and Grandma Lily had grown up with Pops, and the trio had been super close. Both women had been given an open invite to family dinner, ensuring they'd spent quality time with his parents.

"Let's see. I met the second husband but never Benjamin. I remember Opal being a wonderful mother to your Pops. Very welcoming to Lily and me. Sometimes quiet and sad. She loved telling your Pops stories about his adventure loving father, the incredible Benji. I think she still loved the man even though she had remarried."

The poor woman. A victim of the curse, forever doomed to live without her true love. Not that "the incredible Benji" had been so incredible after all. "Did Opal ever mention a woman named Elise Dansing? Or better yet, did you happen to meet Elise, Tiffany Hotchkins's great grandmother?"

"No and no." Fiona tilted her head to the side, her expression thoughtful. "What's this about, hon?"

"Jane hasn't told you?" Conrad piped up, flipping a page of his book. "We're on a treasure hunt. Among other things."

Her cherished friend gasped, grinned and clapped. "We are? Oh! How exciting. Tell me everything!"

With pleasure. "I found a journal written by Benjamin, who believed a former gravekeeper did, in fact, bury gold here. On the night of his disappearance, he thought he'd cracked the code and found the stash. And maybe he did. Maybe he ran off with his newfound wealth, abandoning his wife and child." As well as his (possible) mistress.

"Hmm." Fiona made tsking noises. "I would agree with you, but I doubt a darling woman like Opal would mourn such a sorry excuse of a man so long. Or speak so highly of him."

"Well. I don't think she knew what kind of man he was. He was likely hiding an affair with Elise. Which, as we all know, is the absolute worst crime in the history of mankind. A total betrayal of trust." Thanks to Lily's holiday advice, Jane knew her grandmother would agree.

Perhaps, though, Jane's earlier suspicions had a higher likelihood of success than she'd theorized. Benjamin could have found the gold and met up with Elise, thinking to skip town together. Then Elise killed him, stole his gold, covered up the crime and spent a fortune that rightly belonged to Opal.

"Well I'll be. A secret affair." Fiona shook her head, clearly saddened. "What a scoundrel."

"Agreed. But this particular scoundrel left us clues in his journal," Jane said. "Tell me if these terms mean anything to you. Ready? Here goes. Wailing milk."

Fiona pursed her lips and shook her head.

"Mule easel."

Another shake.

"Sunken ice naps. Island is gall. Inhaled mist."

Her friend started nodding.

A thrum of excitement sparked inside Jane. "You've got something?"

"Maybe." Wide-eyed, the dear woman set her knitting needles aside. "Island is gall is prodding at me."

Oh, oh! They needed to strike while the iron was hot. "Team Truth assemble!" she called, pumping her fist toward the ceiling. "We can figure this out together, I know we can. I'll grab the whiteboard from the office and a couple of markers."

As she flew into action, Conrad placed a bookmark in his book rather than earmarking the page. Wow. She admired him even more. But that was neither here nor there. In less than two minutes, the three of them stood before the board as Fiona wrote each phrase in bright green ink.

She circled the word gall, then tapped it with the end of the marker. "This word is the key."

Jane's lips twisted. "No one with the last name of Gall is buried here. I even checked known causes of death to see if gallbladder showed up. Nothing."

But Fiona appeared unperturbed. If anything, she seemed even more triumphant. "You know that Lily, Pops and I all went to school together. Gary, your pops, loved puzzles and creating codes. All you Ladlings do. I think he was the first kid to earn his morse code badge by the age of nine. On rainy days when we had inside recess, he'd rewrite our names using ciphers or turn them into anagrams. In fact, that's how he proposed to your grandma. He turned the phrase 'Marry me, Lily" into 'My lil ram Rye."

"Ohhhh. Anagrams," Jane said, a light beginning to dawn.

Fiona nodded with enthusiasm. "She loved it so much, she tried to turn his name into an anagram. Called him Dray Galling. She didn't have Gary's flare, but she gave it her best shot. When you mentioned *island is gall*, memories started coming to me, since Gall is part of an anagram for Ladling. In case you're curious, with my maiden name of Drake, Gary dubbed me Adora Knife, which sounds like a bona fide superhero to me."

Yes, yes, yes! More excitement sparked through Jane, creating an inferno. Everything made so much sense. She kissed the other woman's cheek. "You are indeed a super-hero. And a genius!"

Conrad peered at the board, with his head tilted to the side. "So, we need to figure out which Ladling."

"One older than Benjamin," Fiona added. "There are just so many."

"No need. I've already unscrambled the letters." Jane snatched up the red pen and wrote Silas Ladling on the board. The first person buried in the cemetery.

Grinning, Fiona clapped her hands. "You did it! And on your first try. Seems like there are two geniuses in this room. Three, if we grade Conrad on a curve."

He snorted. "Funny."

Jane settled back on her heels, some of her excitement fading. "My immense brain power aside, this is looking like an old mystery already solved. Remember when Beau and I dug up Silas Ladling's grave after the gold rumors resurfaced again…um, allegedly dug up his grave," she added for the former agent's benefit. "There wasn't any gold in his casket."

"That doesn't necessarily mean the gold was found. It could mean the names themselves are clues, rather than spots where the gold was stored," Conrad said.

Oh! "Yes! Of course."

Fiona's grin made a reappearance as she patted his shoulder. "Well. Look who just joined the high IQ club?"

Didn't take Jane long to identify the other names.

Mule easel—Samuel Lee
Barreling dads gin—Dr. Gabriel Dansing. Jane ground her teeth. Another relative of Tiffany's.
Inhaled mist—Daniel Smith
Wailing milk—William King
Sunken ice naps—Sueann Pickens
Bury handgun rod—Rhonda Burgundy

Fiona's phone buzzed, and she winced as she scanned her text. "Uh-oh. I promised Raymond I'd check in on him an hour ago. He's getting antsy. I better go."

"Yes, of course," Jane repeated, already shooing her friend toward the door. "Go take care of our beloved sheriff."

"I feel like things were just getting good, though." The older lady clucked her tongue before wagging her brows. "Granted, the same can also be said of Raymond."

With a groan, Jane plucked Fiona's coat off the hook. Conrad, ever the gentleman, claimed the garment and held it open for the older woman to slide her arms through the sleeves.

Fiona paused at the door. "Oh, Conrad, I just thought of the perfect home for you. My friend Beverly told me that her son, Tucker, is about to sell his house. Can you believe it? Spending three years restoring it to its former glory only to be relocated by his job. Anyway, it's a 1930s art deco, so it will probably remind you of your apartment in Atlanta. There's an in-home theater and outdoor kitchen containing a built-in gas grill. Plus a towel warmer in the bathroom and head-to-toe shower jets."

Lose her roommate so soon? And to the wrong home? "No way." Jane shook her head. "He doesn't want to live in a house with a pool. Think of the maintenance. You'd hate that," she assured him.

Fiona's hand flew to her mouth to cover a sudden cough.

"Jane's right. The maintenance," Conrad said, clearly trying not to grin for some reason. He raised his arms over his head to stretch. The hem of his T-shirt rose over the waist of his low hanging jeans, revealing a patch of his bronze abs.

Mmm. If he wasn't just the tastiest snack in the house...

He snapped his fingers at Cheddar, who still reclined on the couch, jerking Jane from her illicit thoughts. "Let's go, boy. Potty then bedtime." The former agent paused and shook his head in wonder, muttering to himself, "Wow. Not a sentence I ever thought I'd say." He didn't wait to see if the dog felt like obeying or not; he simply walked off, expecting the precious to follow. Which he did.

Rolex prowled behind the pair, as if stalking his prey, and nothing, anywhere, in any period of time, had ever been cuter.

"Goodnight, ladies," her roommate called as he led his good boy toward the back door. Did he feel Jane's eyes upon him?

"Goodnight, Conrad." She didn't want to say she watched his backside as he moved off. No, she certainly did not ever want to say it out loud.

"Jane Ladling," Fiona chided softly, swiping up a ball of yarn and batting it in her direction. "You are stripping that boy with your gaze, and I'm not having it. Not after you broke his sweet, darling heart when you ended things."

Cheeks red, she forced her attention on her friend. "Yes, ma'am. But, um, I didn't break his heart. How could I? You've seen him. He's already over me!"

Fiona spread her arms and gaped at her. "Over you? Sweet goodness. How can you see so much and so little at the same time? That man has got himself more feelings than I ever realized. Hello, he's living in your house and adopted that dog you insisted he needed. I don't mean to spoil your surprise, but honey, everything he's doing, he's doing to win you for the long haul."

What? No! Surely not. He wouldn't...she couldn't... That ...that...made no sense! Did it? "If that's what he's doing–"

"It is. And I'm rooting for him. Maybe a part of you is too? Tell me you're reading Lily's letters, at least."

"I am. But Conrad isn't trying to win me." He couldn't be.

"He is," Fiona insisted.

She swallowed a groan. "Well, if he is, he'll fail." She would make sure of it. For his own good.

THE NEXT MORNING, Jane planned to sit down with Conrad and chat about things. His intentions. His feelings. The curse. Except, when she woke up at 5:00 a.m. to start breakfast, he and Cheddar were already gone. She checked her phone while brewing coffee. Nothing.

Was he handling the Case of the Heisted Hearse solo? But, but… Why not shoot his new roommate a quick message? If he cared for her at all, he would have texted her, yes? Perhaps they didn't need to have that chat, after all.

Sighing, she straightened up the cottage and performed her morning rounds. And, yeah, okay, she might have checked her phone a dozen more times. Still nothing from Conrad.

No matter. Jane turned her attention to Benjamin's list of names. She stopped by all seven gravesites, starting with Samuel Lee, aka mule easel and the first name on the list. Nothing appeared unusual.

Conrad must be right. The names were more than anagrams; they were clues. Clues within clues within clues. But clues to what, exactly?

Could 'mule easel' point to artwork featuring a donkey? Hmmm, should she stop by the library or the museum to search? But how would said artwork relate to Mr. Lee, the cemetery or the hunt for gold? Wrong angle?

Perhaps another clue was hidden somewhere around Mr. Lee's gravesite?

Not knowing what else to do, she cleared wilted and

weather-bleached flower arrangements from his plot. What she didn't do? Consider Conrad and what he might be doing...well, not the whole time.

She moved on to the next grave and the next, doing the same. Thoughts rolling and rolling. Was this a clue? Was that a clue? Hours passed. And oh wow, the sun started sinking low on the horizon, darkness quickly replacing light. She'd spent the day outside, depriving Rolex of the pets he deserved. Less importantly, she hadn't eaten. And where was Conrad? Why hadn't he returned from...whatever he was doing?

Streaked with dirt, she headed to the front of the property and closed the gate, barring visitors. Then she aimed for the cottage. Pleasure surged when she spotted the former agent on the porch, waiting for her despite the chilly breeze. He stood, leaning against the banister, wearing faded jeans and a tight, short sleeve T-shirt that revealed his tattoos. He'd always looked amazing in a suit, but casual fried the circuits in her brain.

"You must be freezing," she said after swallowing a sudden lump in her throat.

He came down the stairs to stand before her. "You're the one who's been out in the elements all day."

She waved her hand. "I'm used to it. When, um, did you get home? Not that I spent the day wondering where you were or anything."

"A little after five," he said, the corners of his mouth twitching.

Her jaw slackened. Hours ago, yet she hadn't noticed. "Where did you—" Her stomach rumbled, protesting the lack of sustenance. Her cheeks flushed. "Um. As I was saying... uh..." What had she been saying?

"Come on." He stretched out his arm. He didn't touch her,

but he didn't change his mind and pull away, either. "Let's feed you. I'll explain where I was while you eat."

Unable to stop herself, she slid her hand in his. She only realized what she'd done when his long fingers laced with hers. A total couple thing to do. But disengage? As if. Tonight, she simply didn't have the strength to fight her attraction to him. She'd resume the battle tomorrow.

"Where are the children?" she asked, not finding any sign of Rolex or Cheddar as Conrad led her from the porch to the kitchen.

"Cheddar is sleeping on my bed, and I last spotted Rolex sitting on my dresser, watching him. It was creepy," he said at the same time she smiled and rasped, "So adorable."

Chuckling, he released her, but only to help her sit upon a barstool. Such a gentlemanly thing to do, but also far too smolder-y for his own good. And if smolder-y wasn't a word, it should be.

"You are the adorable one." He gifted her with a soft smile before tweaking her chin and striding to the refrigerator.

She sucked in a breath. "Am I about to sample your famous cinnamon sugar french toast?"

"You are...not." He withdrew two kinds of cheese, butter and peach jam from the fridge.

She pouted as he set the items on the counter.

He retrieved bread from the box and said, "You're getting an almost as amazing grilled cheese sandwich."

Okay. All right. Not a bad substitute. "You aren't going to eat with me?" she asked when he poured a single glass of sweet tea and passed it her way.

"I ate all of yesterday's diner leftovers as soon as I got home."

She cut off a dreamy whimper. He considered the cottage his home?

Conrad added a generous dollop of butter to her cast iron skillet. "I spoke with the deputy again, but this time I did it in his office, with his files present. He remembered seeing the hearse but he didn't recall noticing anything out of the ordinary."

"And you believed him?"

"For now, I have no reason to doubt him." As the butter sizzled, he added a slice of bread and grated creamy cheese on top. "I spoke with a second deputy on duty that day, just in case he's the one with the crush on you, but he's in his fifties and soon to celebrate his thirty-sixth wedding anniversary."

"As if that would stop him," she teased with a prim tone. A delicious scent filled her kitchen, and she breathed deep.

Conrad flashed her a smile as he slathered the second piece of bread with the jam and placed it in the skillet. "Before the deputies, I was with Adaline Crema."

The woman ticketed the day of Jane's accident.

"She promised to answer any questions I had," Conrad continued, "as long as Cheddar and I drove her on her errands today. Which began at four o'clock in the morning, by the way. She wanted to provide us both with a decent meal before we got started so we'd grow a little fat on our bones."

"Your bones are perfect just as they are," she told him, then flushed again. "Cheddar's too."

He shifted his focus away from the food and onto her. "Perfect?"

Her stomach grumbled again, saving her from having to think up an answer.

"I better finish this before you get hangry," he said, flipping the sandwich over to brown the other side.

She opened her mouth to protest. Lily Ladling's granddaughter would never, ever, *never* get hangry, but that might skirt the edge of flirting. This late-night snack was already too intimate for comfort.

*Focus on the case.* "Where did you take Ms. Crema?" A woman known for her commanding disposition.

At first, Jane thought his heavy sigh would be her only answer. "Everywhere," he finally said. "Absolutely everywhere."

She snickered, and he laughed outright. It was the rustiest, most beautiful sound she'd ever heard, and she ached to hear it again and again and again until his funny bone no longer sounded neglected.

Was Fiona right? Did this man have feelings for her or not?

What was Jane going to do about it, if so?

She swallowed a mouthful of tea, almost choking as it threatened to go down the wrong pipe. "So. Did you learn anything during all this driving around?"

"I did. I learned the feisty bat has a granddaughter named Valerie, who happens to be a little younger than me, is more beautiful than I can ever deserve, and is a super smart general practitioner. But I don't have to worry, because Miss Valerie is nothing like the monsters at Aurelian Hills Medical Clinic."

AHMC, the very clinic Jane visited when sick. And yes, two of the three bodies she'd discovered here at the cemetery had occurred at the hand of an AHMC employee. She'd considered searching for a new doctor, but dang it, they were the only place in town in-network with her insurance, and there was no way she was paying out-of-network rates.

Conrad scooped the sandwich out of the skillet with a spatula, turned off the stove and set the plate before her.

"So, um, are you going to call the beautiful Valerie?" she asked, picking at the crust of her sandwich as she waited for it to cool.

Coming around the counter, he sat in the barrel back chair beside her. He arched a brow. "Should I?"

The question hung in the air between them. She gulped another swig of tea.

After a few tense moments, he showed mercy, forging ahead without pushing. "Adaline noticed the hearse, too. She remembered seeing a heavyset man with a mustache, wearing grease-stained overalls, shut the hood and walk away, as if he'd just finished repairing something for you."

Well. This heavyset man with a stache wanted Jane dead. Why? What had she ever done to him?

Needing to do something with her hands, she grabbed the sandwich and took a bite. Oh wow. Delicious!

"Do you know anyone who fits the description?" Conrad asked, his tone gentle.

She flipped through a variety of mental files, but came up blank. "I do not." She chewed on her bottom lip. "So where does our investigation go from here?"

"I'll visit local mechanics and ask the surrounding shop employees if they remember seeing our guy. Trust me, sweetheart. I'm not going to stop until I find him."

Tremors erupted in her limbs. He'd called her sweetheart again. What did this mean? Something? Nothing?

What did she want it to mean?

# CHAPTER FIVE

Golden rings are always prettier with diamonds. And rubies. And sapphires. And emeralds. And presented in a velvet lined box. But it's the man on bended knee, looking up at you with a heart full of love that is the real prize.

–Lily Ladling's Holiday Advice for Ladies Cursed in Love

*A*s Thanksgiving approached, Jane found no answers. Not for the gold hunt. Not for the car trouble. And certainly not for Conrad's intentions toward her. Or her intentions toward him.

"You're doing it again," her companion said.

She blinked into focus. She kept pace with Beau as he pushed their shopping cart down aisle four of the Golden Food Market, the best and only grocery store in Aurelian Hills. With its lemon-colored laminate flooring, every path looked like a yellow brick road.

"Doing what?" she asked.

"Thinking about Conrad."

She tossed Beau a wry smile before claiming four packets of dry yeast. "He's very thinkaboutable. But to be fair, I was also lamenting the fact that I haven't found Benjamin's gold or the guy who messed with my car."

As they exited the aisle, curving into the next, a pretty cashier waved at Beau. He nodded, giving her a stiff incline of his chin. What he didn't do? Seize the opportunity to flirt and win himself a date.

The cashier's crestfallen face told a story of pure disappointment.

Jane heaved a sigh. How could anyone be so clueless? At least Beau was hot to trot, a feat he pulled off effortlessly despite being such a big, rugged guy. At least six feet four of solid muscle mass.

He might be the brother of her heart but come on! No one couldn't not notice the heat he packed under his skin. Today he wore a Peach State Security T-shirt paired with black work pants.

"You could be missing the chance to meet your soul mate," she told him. "That cashier practically knocked out her cash drawer to catch your attention, and what did you do? Nod. I know you're excited to meet Eunice Park and all, but it's nice to have options in case things don't work out."

As a fledgling matchmaker, on top of being an all but professional sleuth, Jane had scoured social media pages for days, searching for Beau's perfect match. She'd then phoned Eunice, a girl from her graduating class, to set up a double dates. Beau and Eunice, Jane and Conrad. Except, Eunice had never returned her calls. Only a matter of time, though. Surely.

"I'm sure I'll like Eunice just fine," he assured her with a dry tone.

"Who says I'm worrying about you liking her?" she asked

with a wink. "Not only does most of the town trust her with their tax returns, but she volunteers at a local animal shelter." Oh! Maybe she could find a nice pet for Beau. Conrad had Cheddar and look how great that had turned out for him. "As we wait for her to get back with me, you should work on your flirting game...and I should find you someone else. Yes, that's exactly what I'll do."

He groaned. "Please don't."

"Too late. I already have ideas." Unless... "Ohhhh. I think I get it now. You're keeping yourself free for Sora Khatri." The mysterious woman Jane and Fiona had discovered hiding out in his apartment for her "protection." Jane had detected a touch of loneliness about the sassy woman. Like she needed a friend.

Hmmm. What was Sora doing for Thanksgiving, now that the threat of danger was over?

Beau's next groan proved louder. "How is Conrad's hunt for a place to live?" he asked, changing the subject. "I think I've talked to him about everything but that."

"Honestly? It's not going well." He'd asked her about multiple homes, but she had yet to recommend a walk-through. They were just too...wrong. Wrong neighborhood, wrong size, wrong vibe. So, the search continued.

"And so the two of you continue living together." Did she detect a snicker in his tone? "How is having a roommate?"

"Wonderful and terrible and amazing and awful." She grabbed three boxes of rice and tossed them in the basket, then adjusted the mini top hat she'd paired with her black and white dress. Jane planned to prepare a holiday feast the likes of which her guests had never seen. "He takes out the trash, gets things from top shelves for me, and washes dishes. He doesn't get in my way. In fact, I think he sometimes actively avoids me to give me my space."

"Yes, that does sound terrible," he told her, using an even drier tone than before.

"Thank you! Finally someone agrees with me," she replied, choosing to ignore his sarcasm. If he didn't mean it, he shouldn't say it. "We've been super friendly with each other." But she wasn't sure she'd ever been more miserable. "I hate the Ladling curse so much."

He didn't respond right away, his expression pensive. "I'll be honest. I agree with him. I think the curse is only true because you believe it." Beau shot out his arm and snagged a package of soft, orange circus peanuts, and tossed it in the cart. "If anyone could break it, though, it's Conrad. That man might have you beat in the stubborn department."

One could hope. Wait, had Beau called her stubborn?

"He's even making progress on the hearse case," he said.

"He is?" Her heart rate sped up. "He hasn't mentioned anything to me."

Her companion blanched. "Maybe I misspoke?"

Jane paused to prop a hand on her hip. "Beauregard Harden, you tell me what theory he's pursuing right this second or so help me, I'll call up Sora myself and set up a *series* of double dates."

He lifted a brow again, this time in challenge. "Oh yeah? Who are *you* bringing?"

Yep, that one stung. "Who says I'll be there? These double date will be with you and Sora and Fiona and Sheriff Moore."

Her brother of the heart lifted his hands in surrender. "Conrad's identified the mechanic who screwed with the pipes. He's narrowed down who paid—"

"What?"

Unease filtered over his expression, and he scrubbed a hand over his beautiful face. "No, you know what? If he hasn't told you about it, he has a good reason. I won't be telling you anything else, I don't care what you threaten."

Oh really? "Please know this will pain you far more than it pains me, but it's got to be done. Your punishment is the silent treatment. Five—two!—whole minutes of it."

He stopped in the middle of the aisle and pretended to stab himself in the heart.

She stopped too. "You brought this on yourself. Also, the clock hasn't started yet. Obviously."

"Shouldn't I be rewarded for my integrity?" he asked, hopeful.

Leaning in, she told him, "Why do you think I deducted three minutes?"

His broad shoulders slumped in faux dejection, but only for a moment. He straightened and narrowed his eyes. "Guess what? I'm giving you the silent treatment too."

"As if! What crime have I committed?"

"You stole my common sense," he accused. "There is no other reason I would be in an argument about the silent treatment."

"Ha! The judge just threw out your case for lack of evidence. Which means the argument is over, and I won. Anything else you add from this point forward is the start of a new one. So. The best you can do now is break me, and we both know that's impossible. Now come on. The groceries won't jump into my cart on their own. Get to fetching."

In the promised silence, she collected another item she needed for the, admittedly, elaborate menu she'd chosen. Besides the traditional roasted turkey and ham, cornbread dressing, mashed potatoes and gravy, sweet potato casserole with marshmallows, butternut squash soup, green bean casserole, broccoli and rice casserole, jalapeño popper mac 'n cheese, the world's best deviled eggs, all the greens and cole slaw, there'd be half a dozen different pies, a few cakes, and cookies. Probably a pudding and a sticky toffee too.

"Oh, I think I know how I can get you to talk to me before time is up," he said, twenty seconds into his required two minutes.

She pressed her lips firmly together, projecting a challenge. *Try me.*

"Is there a perfect hat for my face type?" Beau asked.

Ack! The question was so, so good, an answer nearly snuck past her tongue. Yes! A black, flat-topped pilgrim's hat, complete with buckle. But she gripped the basket tighter to keep from blurting out her answer.

"We both know you love dressing me up," he said next. "Tell me a costume, any costume, no matter how grotesque, tight or emasculating, and I'll wear it to Thanksgiving dinner. But only if you tell me right this second."

Gah! Another doozy. He would make the perfect turkey, complete with red, yellow and brown feathers. Except, Jane was a woman of her word, dang it, with a stubborn streak like no other. She pretended to concentrate on her shopping list instead.

"That didn't do it, hmm?" he said, sounding shocked.

Okay, so, this definitely hurt her more than it hurt him. Finally her mental punishment countdown clock ran out and she blurted, "You've earned a penalty!" The words exploded from her.

"What'd I do this time?" he demanded.

"You taunted the darling woman who's only trying to teach you valuable life lessons. Such as spilling all secrets to her always. But don't worry, you won't suffer with my silence this time. I—Wait! I just remembered something I need a few aisles over. Be a dear and grab me a box of wool tampons with wings. I'll be right back."

As he stood there, blinking at her, she rushed off with the

cart to fetch…something. Anything to hide the smile attempting to grow over her face. *Good luck with your search, tiger.*

Oh, lookie there. Limited edition pumpkin pie biscuits for pets. She grabbed two boxes. The little sugars in her life should have a holiday feast of their own.

"Jade Ladling!" A familiar female voice rang out. "Agent Ryan said you'd be here."

She sucked in a breath and spun. "Tiffany Hotchkins."

The widow stormed over, tennis shoes squeaking on the yellow laminate. Never had she appeared so rumpled. Dark hair falling from a sloppy bun. Shirt wrinkled and stained beneath her coat, and loose pajama pants. A purse dangled from one arm. She held a yellowed sheet of paper.

"I was so desperate to prove you wrong," she lamented the second she paused in front of Jane. "I dug through storage, tore apart the attic as well as the basement, and searched every box of family heirlooms. I even contacted distant relatives to collect whatever they had. You know what I found?" Tiffany waved the paper between them. "Letters."

"Is that potato chip dust in your hair?" Jane asked.

"Your stupid great grandfather wrote to my great grandmother. They talked about running away and raising the baby together. What if the baby was his, Jane?" she shrieked. "What if we are, in fact, related?"

Oh…yikes. Affair between Benjamin and Elise confirmed. Wild speculation about being distantly related to a mortal enemy likely.

"They also talked about his hunt for gold," Tiffany continued at a softer volume. Her eyes narrowed with speculation. "That *is* why you're doing this, isn't it? You aren't going after my family fortune. You're going after your own. Which might also be mine."

"Jane," Beau called, saving her from having to think up a response.

Both Tiffany and Jane whipped toward him. He stood at the end of the aisle, holding two different boxes of tampons, not the least bit embarrassed. "Neither is wool, and there's nothing with wings. You okay with organic? And do you want super plus or small?"

What she wanted to do was to go back in time and shake some sense into her great grandfather Benjamin. Barring that, she'd have to settle for finding his gold.

# CHAPTER SIX

Geese aren't the smartest of animals but even they know to
get to a-laying and start a family

–Lily Ladling's Holiday Advice for Ladies Cursed in Love

*J*ane parked her hearse in front of the cottage,
next to a compact SUV she didn't recognize.
Great. A mysterious visitor when she needed to
focus on finding Benjamin's treasure, ensuring Tiffany didn't
beat her to it. The very reason Jane had made a brief stop at
the museum on the way home. Just a two second pop in to
ask an employee about any donkey art, and yes, she'd
dragged Beau along. Turned out to be a dead end, unfortunately.

She spotted an older woman sitting on a porch rocker.
Not someone she'd ever encountered before. And also not
the rocker where she'd found the body of poor Ana Irons.

That one had been donated to charity after a thorough cleaning.

"I'll handle the groceries," Beau said, unbuckling. "You handle the intruder."

"You mean you aren't going to frisk her for weapons first?" she teased, then tsked under her tongue. "Wow. Slacking on the job, Harden. And to think, you usually go the extra mile."

He snorted. "I think you can handle a little old lady."

They both emerged into the chilly afternoon. Jane hurried up the steps, approaching the visitor, who had a curly cap of salt and pepper hair. "Hello. I'm the owner and operator of Garden of Memories. How may I help you?"

"Hello." A warm, sunny smile bloomed, erasing ten years from the guest's age. "I'm Susan Albertson. You must be Jane."

"Yes. That's me. I am she. Her. No, I'm pretty sure it's she." She offered a little wave. "How may I help you?"

Beau strode past them carrying what looked to be a thousand cloth sacks of groceries at once, making Jane think she should insist he tag along on every shopping excursion from now on. He nodded to Ms. Albertson, saying, "Ma'am." By some miracle, he managed to open the front door before Jane could rush over to help.

"I came to see Conrad," Susan said.

Instant mind whirls, with thoughts colliding into each other. "Stella isn't here, so I'm guessing he's out running errands." Wait. Did Susan know Stella? Was she here for business or something personal? Had Conrad known she was coming? "I can take a message for him."

"Oh, there's no need. I already texted him, and he's on his way here. I'm his foster mom, in case you were wondering."

How wonderful! "I'm so happy to meet you." Grinning,

Jane hastened to the woman's side and guided her past the front door. "Please, come in. Let's get you comfortable while you wait for Conrad."

They headed straight to the kitchen, where Beau unpacked and stored the groceries. Jane made introductions as she led Susan to the small round table rather than the more formal one in the dining room, then hurried to the fridge to fix three Mason jars of sweet tea with a sprig of mint.

She spotted Rolex in the windowpane, peering out. A quick glance revealed Cheddar frolicking in the fenced backyard shaded by the branches of an enormous hickory. Beau must have put him out to stretch his legs. And oh, wow, was her kitty ever riveted by the sight. He stared, unblinking.

Cutest bromance of all time!

Jane settled at the table with Susan and slid a glass her way. Beau drained his jar at the counter rather than joining them.

"Ladies," he said then, and left as quickly as he'd entered. Probably going to do a quick check of the premises. Or escape an uncomfortable encounter with a stranger. Or both.

"Were you Wyatt's foster mom too?" Wyatt was Conrad's younger brother—either biological or foster, she wasn't sure which. Jane had gotten to meet him the first and only time she'd visited Conrad in the city.

"I was." Susan glanced heavenward, as if praying for divine patience. "Those boys and their troubles."

"Oh? Do tell."

Another smile bloomed. "Conrad mentioned you might have questions for me." Her expression turned thoughtful. "He also informed me I had permission to answer whatever you asked."

Really, truly? Her heart skipped a beat. What did that

GENA SHOWALTER & JILL MONROE

mean, though? Why would he do such a generous thing for an ex-girlfriend? He'd always been so closed off about his past. "Well, I only have one question. More of a request, really."

"Go ahead. I'm ready."

Okay then. "Tell me absolutely everything you know about him. Leave nothing out. No detail is too small. I'm so curious about young Conrad. And older Conrad, if I'm being honest."

Sadness suddenly pulsed from her. "I only got to spend about eight months with him. Not nearly long enough. After losing his family in a car accident, he bounced between foster homes. He went from shock to grief to anger, as you can imagine, and began to lash out. Or so I was told. He went to a group home for trouble boys and stayed there until the age of fifteen, when he came to live with me. He'd only just begun to come out of his shell when he asked me to relinquish him."

Then. That moment. Jane's heart shattered into hundreds of tiny pieces. Young Conrad...somber... "Why did he ask to be relinquished?"

"He wanted Wyatt, who is several years younger, to live with me. The two met in the group home, but Wyatt wasn't doing well there. Conrad knew I had room for only one charge at a time. He asked me to take Wyatt instead. I made a few inquiries, and Wyatt came to live with me soon after Conrad left, and he stayed until he aged out of the system. They both come to visit me several times a year."

Those sweet, darling boys. Had they felt rejected in different homes, unwanted by other families? Were they bullied by other kids? Did they find any happiness? Tears welled in Jane's eyes.

"Is Wyatt his biological brother?" Best to make sure.

"No." Susan tilted her head. "You love Conrad, don't you?" Her eyes widened as soon as the words left her mouth, and

64

she pressed a hand over her mouth. "I'm sorry. That's the one topic I wasn't supposed to mention, no matter what."

Jane jerked, almost knocking her jar of tea to the ground. In love with Conrad? No, no. Of course not. With shaky legs, she rose and darted to the refrigerator to cover her awkwardness. She wrenched open the magnet-covered door, allowing the chilly fridge air to cool her overheated cheeks.

Conrad had spoken of Jane with the woman he most likely thought of as his second mother. Not only had he brought up the subject of love, but he'd also set perimeters. For Jane's comfort? An amazingly thoughtful gesture.

*You love him, don't you?*

Her throat tightened. "I don't love him. I can't." *But I wish I had the freedom to do so.*

Ugh. Grandma Lily's letters must be getting to her.

Hinges squeaked in the distance, alerting Jane to a new arrival. Her pulse spiked at the sound of heavy footsteps. Familiar footsteps. Tremors swept through her limbs, but she managed to close the door to the fridge without toppling. Conrad entered the kitchen a second later, his broad shoulders filling the doorframe.

He met her gaze and immediately tensed. His expression... he looked as if he'd just taken a punch to the stomach. "What's wrong?" he demanded, zooming over to run his fingers down her arm as if assessing her for an injury. He glanced at Susan. "What's wrong with her?"

That his first instinct was to comfort and protect only quadrupled Jane's guilt. Yes, guilt. This man... He deserved an amazing girlfriend. Someone unafraid of love, who would devote herself to ensuring he received all the affection he'd missed as a child.

She swallowed a barbed lump in her throat. If she were truly his friend, as she claimed, she would matchmake for him, just like she did with Beau, and find him the perfect partner. Could she?

"Nothing's the matter." Jane gave his hand a reassuring squeeze, wishing she could throw herself against his chest and hug him. "I'm just glad you're home, that's all."

He tucked a strand of her hair behind her ear, allowing his thumb to continue to stroke the wayward lock. A moment later, he stopped with a jerk, as if realizing what his actions spelled out for everyone in the room.

He still cared about her.

Before she could panic, he melted her with a slow, confident smile and drew her closer, tucking her against his side. Too weak to protest, she leaned against him and breathed in his scent. Because of the curse, they could never be a couple. Because of her greedy heart, she doubted she could pair him with someone else. But. She might have to force herself to do it. In the meantime, she could and would give him good memories of a loving family, friends and holidays filled with warmth and cheer… before saying goodbye after Christmas.

Yes. The smartest path. The only route able to save his life and her heart.

Releasing him required every ounce of her willpower, but she did it. Jane turned to Susan. "Please come and celebrate Thanksgiving with us on Thursday. You and Wyatt. Beau will be here. And maybe three of his–our–friends." Perhaps she could even locate Beau's mysterious lady friend Sora.

"Oh, I would love to," Susan said, "but I've already agreed to spend Thanksgiving with my sister and her family."

No matter. Jane refused to be deterred. "You're coming, right?" she asked Conrad.

"There's nowhere else I'd rather be." His eyes glinted with amusement. "I'll even help you cook."

Heart thudding, she intoned, "Excellent. Well. Now that that's settled, I'll leave you two alone to talk. I've got a treasure to find, after all." After offering an *I'm-completely-harm-less* smile to both Susan and Conrad, she rushed to the stairs.

"Jane," he called, but she didn't respond.

She shut herself inside her bedroom and leaned against the door, already mentally exhausted. It was decided. She would, in fact, find Conrad his perfect woman to love and cherish. His own personal treasure.

# CHAPTER SEVEN

Swans a-swimming are so graceful, elegant and lovely.
Reminds me of a bride on her wedding day. And like two
swans in love who press their heads together, forming a
heart, a husband and wife twine their fingers, forming a
bond.

–Lily Ladling's Holiday Advice for Ladies Cursed in Love

*T*he next morning, the day before
Thanksgiving, Jane awoke with a new purpose.
Forget that she might be related to Tiffany. According to the
Headliner, Ms. Hotchkins had left town to be with family.
Meaning, there'd be no more surprise confrontations. Jane
planned to take full advantage.

Today she hunted for gold *and* a girlfriend for Conrad.
Yes, she was very aware of her nonexistent success record
with matchmaking, but she was determined to get this right.
Who better to succeed with than Conrad? He deserved a

good woman. The best. Something Jane would fight to ensure he got. Because that's what good friends did for each other.

In fact, she'd start with this most noble of quests.

She licked suddenly dry lips and knocked on his bedroom door. Rolex came dashing over to join her.

Cheddar barked from behind the barricade. A groan followed. "Is this business or pleasure, Jane?"

"Pleasure. But also business. Mostly business."

Another groan. "Come back in a few hours then."

Oh no! Was Conrad sick? He'd sounded sick. Concern swamped her, and she knocked with more force. "I'm coming in on the count of three to take your temperature," she informed him. "Be ready." Or not. "One."

"It's too early for business," he mumbled.

Too early? She double checked the time on her phone and frowned. "It's barely five a.m., and our Thanksgiving desserts aren't going to bake themselves. Besides, we haven't gotten to spend much time together lately, so we're overdue for a chat. Therefore, if you aren't coming down with a debilitating disease, I expect you to be in the kitchen in twenty minutes or less. Or else!"

With a firm nod, she marched downstairs to gather everything they would need. Ingredients. Bowls. Measuring cups. Aprons. She selected a darling retro red polka-dotted apron with white ruffles for herself and tied the strings, telling Rolex, "Mommy loves you, but you aren't allowed to help with this, only watch."

The furry gift to humanity hopped in his centerpiece bowl atop the dining room table.

Conrad joined them—on time—looking rumpled and adorable with messy hair, hooded eyes and a black T-shirt, the cuffs stretched around his biceps. What the man did for gray sweatpants should be criminal. She was already

GENA SHOWALTER & JILL MONROE

perspiring, and the oven hadn't even started pre-heating yet.

Half asleep, he said, "Let me take Cheddar outside before we start."

He led the darling canine past her, padding to the back yard. Cheddar's little orange and white tush swished back and forth as he waddled, and Jane smiled. Animals made everything better.

The two returned a few minutes later. Conrad fed his furson, then approached Jane, smelling of fresh air and clean, cotton sheets.

"Reporting for duty, sir," he said, saluting her.

Grinning, she tied a black apron with frilly purple pockets around his waist, then stepped back to admire him. Hmm, the lavender embroidered *Good Lookin' is Cookin'* might be a little too on point, but how perfect was he?

Wait. Hold up. Better stop that runaway train in its tracks. There would be no admiring him today of all days.

"Why did we need to be up so early to make a pumpkin pie?" he asked, scrubbing a hand down the back of his neck and eyeing the staircase as if thinking of returning to bed. "I'll grab a tub of whipped cream from the store and we're more than halfway done."

She raised a brow at him. "I hope you're not suggesting a lone pie, great though it is, will suffice? It's like you don't even know me? And did the idea of store bought whipped cream come out of your filthy mouth? In the presence of a lady no less? We will be whipping the cream ourselves and–"

Conrad's shoulders began to shake with laughter, and she knew she'd been had. Riling her up was payback for waking him so early. The man might know her better than anyone. He–oh, no, no, no. Not this again.

Jane whirled around to grab her recipe cards and distract herself from Mr. Good Lookin' and his teasing. "In addition to the pumpkin pie and homemade whipped cream, we're baking sticky toffee cake, butter cake, a mincemeat pie, as well as pecan, apple, and custard respectively. We'll also be making pumpkin cream cheese cookies and turkey-shaped brownies for Fiona's grandkids."

A delightfully dazed expression spread over his face. "I thought they weren't coming."

"They aren't. We're sending the treats to them," she informed him.

He tapped the end of her nose. "I think someone just wants pumpkin cream cheese cookies and turkey shaped brownies for herself."

Jane shrugged. "I mean, if a few end up on our Thanksgiving Day table, that can't be helped." And oh, wow, was this going to be a totally different holiday than usual.

Before, Jane had celebrated with Fiona, her two children and their families. This time, Fiona and kin would be accompanying the sheriff to his daughter's, and Jane would be playing hostess to six adults. Conrad. Beau. Trick. Holden. Isaac. And Wyatt. Men with amazing appetites.

Things would be different for Conrad, too. He'd once admitted he had always preferred working on holidays.

"Oh, I forgot to mention," he said. "Wyatt asked if he could bring a date. Also, of all the desserts, I think the sticky toffee will be my favorite. I think we should start with that."

Okay, so, Jane would be playing host to seven adults. "Please tell Wyatt there's plenty of room. And good to know about your favorite. We'll bake that last, so you have something to work toward."

He snorted. "When did you become so cruel, sweetheart?"

Her stomach flipped over. Sweetheart again and with such a warm and rough tone. His new lady love must, must, must be able to draw out this elusive teasing nature of his. And also coax him to smile. And spark his laughter.

"Um. I don't think you should call me that anymore." His future girlfriend wouldn't appreciate it.

He didn't miss a beat. "Ten-four, pancake."

Jane blinked at him. "Excuse me? Did you just call me *pancake?*"

"I did. Because it's your new nickname."

Gah! Did he have to be so danged cute? Trembling, she got real busy real fast and pointed to a recipe. "We'll start with the butter cake. I'll do dry, you do wet."

He got busy mixing eggs and milk. "You mentioned wanting to have a chat?"

"That's right." She dumped flour, sugar and salt together. A cloud of white puffed up from the bowl. Maybe she'd used a little too much force. She waved off the tell-tale proof of her agitation and said, "I have questions, you have answers." Here goes. "What do you look for in a girlfriend? Like, what are your top three must haves?"

Silence greeted her questions. She had enough time to draw a little heart in the flour mixture with her spoon and rush to smooth it out before anyone noticed. Finally, she shifted to glance at him. Had he even heard–

Conrad was staring at her, energy pulsing from him. An electrifying energy that seemed to say, *You are what I look for in a girlfriend. You're my top three must haves.*

Her mouth dried and it took everything inside her not to tremble under the heat radiating from his gaze. No. This simply would not do. If anything, finding Benjamin's journal had only solidified the danger of the curse. Not even Lily's sage advice had helped. Conrad would not suffer under Jane's watch.

"I'm being serious," she told him, adding a smile she didn't feel.

He pursed his lips. "You're matchmaking me, aren't you?"

"Maybe. Trust me, you'll thank me later," she told him with a humph.

Another loaded pause. Then, "I'm seriously kicking myself for not anticipating this, but all right. I'll play along." He slid his bowl her way. As she combined wet with dry, he crossed his arms over his chest, a calculated gleam glowing brighter and brighter in his eyes. "My top three must haves, in order of preference. One." He extended an index finger. "She must be unwaveringly kind, savagely honest, fiercely loyal, and lovingly vicious. But she must also be enchantingly naïve and bafflingly smart in the most illogical ways, with stunning confidence and odd insecurities in equal measure."

Her eyes widened. "That's a *single* requirement?" She shook as she poured cake batter into three pans. "And it's a must have, you say, with absolutely zero wiggle room?" Was there even such an—admittedly amazing sounding—person out there?

"Two," he continued as if she hadn't spoken, holding up a second finger. "If she can't whip up a feast just because, using only the ingredients she has on hand, she's not for me."

Oookay. Talk about random and specific. "Can she at least borrow sugar from a neighbor if necessary?"

Again he continued without acknowledging her question. Lifting another finger, he said, "Third. When I'm with her, I want to feel like I'm part of a family again. As if losing every-thing over and over again wasn't an anchor meant to drown me, but a tool that shaped me into the man this woman needs. Someone who appreciates her quirks, sees the value of her generous heart, and remains unafraid to fight for what he wants. No matter how long it takes."

Jane reeled as she slid the pans into the oven to bake. So much to unpack. The woman he'd just described...the *man* he'd just described. Sweet goodness! No wonder she'd almost fallen in love with him.

She set the timer and shifted to face him with growing reluctance. "I'm gonna be honest with you. I might have better luck creating your ideal partner from a computer program."

"You can't think of *anyone* who might qualify?" he asked, glancing skyward before crossing to the sink to get started on cleaning the dishes they'd dirtied.

"No." And she so wished she could because she longed to be the incomparable woman's friend. Though the friendship would be tough considering said woman was enjoying everything Jane had ever wanted.

She fished out her next recipe, ready to start the batch of pumpkin cream cheese cookies. "What led to your breakups with your past girlfriends?" Her chest clenched as she re-popped the lid on the flour canister. "Besides me, I mean."

A pause. Then, "It's my turn to be honest with you," he said, drying his hands and closing in on her. Heat wafted from him. The scent of him enveloped her.

Her knees trembled. She waited, but he didn't offer any additional information. Or reach for her.

"Yes," she prompted, breathless, looking anywhere but Conrad, "please do be honest with me." The man could be so closed off about himself, which she understood, but this moment felt important, as if the two of them were advancing across a rickety bridge together.

"I will. But first…look at me Jane," he said, his voice tight with an emotion she couldn't define. He leaned his hip against the counter. "I only want to say this once, and I'd rather not declare it to the side of your face."

Her grip tightened on the spoon. She steeled herself before rotating toward him. He captured and searched her gaze. The longing in his dark eyes nearly drove her to her knees.

"I learned a long time ago not to hold on to anyone," he

said. "I'd only hurt worse when they left me. And they always left me."

The statement struck her as one part admission and one part challenge. No doubt losing his family in the car accident and then moving from one foster home to another had seared that lesson into his brain.

"Before us," he continued, "I had never been in a serious relationship. I didn't want to be. I was happiest dating someone casually for a few months, then deciding to move on for some reason or another. No harm, no foul."

She swallowed. "And now?"

The chords of his throat worked, his Adam's apple bobbing up and down. "Now, I'm ready to go all in."

JANE COULDN'T SLEEP that night. Conrad was ready to go all in. With the next woman he dated.

Conrad.

All in.

With someone besides Jane. Maybe even someone she picked for him.

Curses sucked! Needing a distraction, she turned her attention to Benjamin's journal. Mainly, the seven names and a map of the cemetery. The print out of the map she often passed out to visitors. Something about the two items together prodded at her mind, but what? She even marked the seven gravesites on the map, but no pattern emerged. And yet...

Yeah. That *something* never faded. Again and again, just before she could grasp the answer, her thoughts returned to Conrad. She pictured him with the ladies of Aurelian Hills and did not like it. In desperation to fully occupy her mind, she scrolled through Instagram to find a new date for Beau. As late night scrolling often did, it took her down unusual paths. This time, to a page for the vet's former "roommate" Sora Kahtri.

Tons of pictures of the dark-haired beauty's travels populated the feed, though none were recent. And not a single one of her family. Or of any kind of holiday. Sadness tugged at Jane's heart. It was a longshot, but she sent the other woman a direct message, inviting her to Thanksgiving lunch/dinner. Dinch? Lunner?

Despite her lack of sleep, Jane popped up before her alarm sounded, eager to begin her morning of chopping, braising and stuffing the turkey. But not before texting Fiona a holiday meme–*Keep your Thanksgiving food from going bad by eating it all in one day.* Also not before she discovered another shredded hat, courtesy of Rolex. The little scamp! He did love to play.

After a quick wake-up shower, Jane donned a fit-and-flare covered in tiny pancake stacks. A garment reserved for special occasions. Rolex followed her to the kitchen and perched in his centerpiece bowl as she tottered about, stirring and chopping and heating. As the scents of caramelized onion and melting butter scented the air, Conrad came downstairs, looking more rumpled and adorable than ever as he led Cheddar outside. She prepared him a mug of coffee.

"Smells amazing in here," he told her upon his return. "Like my favorite memories."

For once, no sadness tinged his voice when he spoke of the time before he'd lost his family in a tragic accident. Delight puffed up her chest. Maybe, just maybe, she'd helped him think of the past in a new way. Not in all he'd lost, but what he'd once enjoyed.

"And your dress." A grin bloomed as he looked her over.

"The pancake is wearing pancakes. There's nothing more perfect."

What a wonderful compliment. She heard an odd cracking sound—inside herself. "Th-thank you." Trembling, she passed him the coffee.

"No, thank *you*." He sipped the brew and washed dishes while the corgi sat at his feet, gazing up at him with adoration. "Anything I can do to help?" he asked as soon as those dishes were done.

Behind him, Rolex stalked across the kitchen table, closing in, his glare laser focused on the father and his furson. "Entertain my baby? He's eager to play."

Conrad winked at her, and oh, did he give good wink. "Consider it done." With a slight shift, he swooped the feline into his arms, holding the stunned creature with eyes now as wide as saucers against his chest. They exited the kitchen, Cheddar trotting happily behind them.

A dangerous sense of contentment fell over Jane. Rather than going to war with it, letting the dread of finding Conrad a new girlfriend or the unpleasantness of his brand new willingness to commit sweep over her, she made a decision to relish the day. Humming a song from her childhood, she dove into her baking with gusto. The love she couldn't pour into the former agent, she poured into her food.

The landline in the office rang just as she began to whisk the gravy for a surprise sausage, egg and biscuit breakfast casserole. "Would you get that Conrad? And put my phone on the charger while you're in there, please?" All that late night scrolling had drained the battery.

Conrad returned to the kitchen a few minutes later, frowning. No sign of the animals. "That was Trick. Someone hacked into the servers at a bank in Atlanta. He, Holden and Isaac are on their way there now. He's sorry, but they couldn't turn down holiday pay. They'll come as soon as they can, but they'll definitely be late."

"It's all right. We'll make them all a plate."

"Exactly what I told them."

Excellent. But as she refocused on the gravy, it was her turn to frown. The boisterous and jovial found-family atmosphere she'd hoped to create had morphed into an intimate group of five. Two of whom were dating and two of whom used to date. Oh no. Would Beau feel like a fifth wheel?

Had Sora seen Jane's message? Any chance she'd show up?

A knock sounded at her door. Eek! The guests were arriving. She twisted to peer out the kitchen window and spotted Beau's old truck.

"I'll get the door," Conrad called.

A sleek red sports car parked beside the beater. As Wyatt emerged and jogged to the passenger side of the vehicle, excitement bloomed.

"No," she called back. "You get comfortable, and I'll get the door." Jane quickly dried her hands on a dishtowel and hurried to the living room. She must, must, must meet the woman Conrad's fun, lively foster brother was dating.

As she waited in the open entrance for the pair to stride closer, she hugged Beau hello. How amazing he looked in his dress shirt and slacks. Conrad sat on the couch with Cheddar on his lap and Rolex perched just behind his shoulder, glaring. His love language.

Her jaw nearly dropped when the handsome Wyatt escorted a ginger bombshell inside. He shut the door behind her. The newcomer wore a curve-hugging dress of fiery scarlet with a deep V. Mile high stilettos revealed toes painted jet black. Vibrant red lipstick completed the look.

Conrad blinked at her, as if in awe. The only sound came from Beau as he gulped.

The beauty glanced at the former agent before concentrating on Jane. "Hi, I'm Lorelei," she said, extending her hand. "Thank you for inviting me to your home. I planned to bring my famous ambrosia salad, but Wyatt said you'd be insulted if I did."

"Ambrosia salad would have been a wonderful addition to the menu," Jane told her, shaking her head at Wyatt. "In fact, I think I have the ingredients. Why don't you whip up a batch? We can get to know each other while I finish my current dish and start the next." And the next and the next. She had tons of questions for the woman.

Cheddar hopped down and trotted to each guest, seeking pets.

"Wyatt," Conrad grated before Lorelei had a chance to respond. He stood and glared at his foster brother. "A word in private, please."

"Nah, I'm good," the other man replied with a shrug.

Um. What did Conrad wish to discuss? Annoyance and exasperation rolled from him in waves. "This is Beau," she said, "my best friend." Beau and Wyatt shook hands. "I'm assuming you've already met Conrad?" she asked Lorelei.

"Oh, yes." The redhead cast the soon-to-be sheriff another glance, this one lingering. Her voice dropped an octave. "We used to date." Her heels clicked on the hardwood floor as she slinked over to place a kiss on his cheek. "Didn't we, Connie?"

Connie? Startled, Jane glanced at her ex-boyfriend. This was the kind of woman he used to date? Flame haired femme fatales?

"We went on two dates," he said, the grating worse. Lots worse. "Hardly dating."

Wyatt stuffed his hand in his pockets, rocked back on his heels and whistled.

A snicker burst from Beau. "This is going to be my favorite holiday ever. I can already tell."

Another knock sounded at the door, and Jane rushed to open it. Thank goodness. A distraction.

"I decided to take you up on your offer." Sora Kahtri stood on the porch, elegant in a white top and matching pants. Dark skin radiant, chestnut eyes framed by long, curling lashes, and black hair hanging to her waist, curling at the ends, she absolutely stunned. "Is that okay?" she asked.

"Of course." Jane threw her arms around her, giving her guest a welcoming hug. "I'm so glad you came. Please, come in."

Beau began to choke. "What's she doing here?"

"Whatever she wants," Sora snapped at him as she entered behind Jane.

Okay, so the two hadn't really gotten along. But they were definitely intrigued with each other. Even now, they couldn't inched closer.

It was Conrad's turn to snicker. "I agree," he said, patting the vet on the shoulder. "Best holiday ever."

"Happy Thanksgiving, everyone," Wyatt announced, spreading his arms, and Jane would swear Rolex grinned from his perch on the couch.

The wind-up timer announced the rising rolls were ready to be kneaded. "If you'll excuse me." Jane rushed back to the kitchen, thankful to escape.

She spent the rest of the morning and afternoon in the kitchen, baking, baking, baking. Lorelei never showed to mix her salad, but others snuck in and out of the kitchen to snag a taste of this or that. Between those visits, muted arguments filtered her way, and she cringed.

Finally, as she slathered melted butter over the freshly bake rolls, she called, "Who's hungry?"

An unenthusiastic chorus rang out. Seconds later, the

group stalked into the kitchen, their expressions strained. Cheddar did not follow. Avoiding the fuddy duddies? Smart dog. Rolex, who'd worked his way to the top of the refrigerator, hissed and batted at anyone who passed by. Unfortunately, not even his adorable personality could save the mood.

Jane clapped her hands, a schoolteacher taking charge of her students. "Line up, everyone, fill a plate, and settle in at the dining table," she instructed. Maybe full bellies would do the trick.

Conrad waved her over. "Ladies first."

What manners. Taking a place at the counter where all the food was laid out, Jane selected all of her favorite dishes. But as everyone gathered at the table, the atmosphere became even more strained. People picked at their food. The meal she'd looked forward to and planned meticulously had grown into an uneasy affair. Most of her traditional roasted turkey and ham remained on the platter, growing sad. The butternut squash soup remained untouched in the tureen. But it was her cornbread dressing preparing to go soggy in Grandma Lily's china that pushed Jane over the edge.

She flattened her palms on the table. "Did everyone wear their listening ears today?" she demanded. All eyes zoomed her way. "None of you are worthy of my desserts. Or my food! So, leave your plates and grab a coat. Your food is going to chill–and so are you. We're going outside to hunt for gold."

"Outside...in the cemetery?" Lorelei asked with a shudder.

"But the game is on," Wyatt complained, twisting in his chair to glimpse the television screen in the living room. He didn't seem to care that his date was currently making happy-eyes at Conrad, who radiated tension.

The other men made muttering noises of agreement. Sora shrugged.

Steadfast, Jane shook her head. "If it's not the Bulldogs playing, it's not football, as my Pops used to say. So let's go. I'll meet you at the front door and give you your assignments."

Five minutes later, her crew stood by the front door as ordered. "Beau and Sora, you'll be together. Your assignment is to investigate Dr. Gabriel Dansing's headstone, while keeping this phrase in mind. Barreling dads gin."

The two grumbled, but off they went.

"Don't come back until you're smiling," Jane called. She turned to Conrad. "You're with Lorelei." He opened his mouth to protest as the other woman eagerly hooked her arm through his, but Jane shook her head, silencing him. The former daters needed to clear the air. What she knew? He would never make a move on his foster brother's date. "You're searching the gravesite of Sueann Pickens and thinking of sunken ice naps. I'm working with Wyatt." She smiled at Conrad's brother—who was about to get a stern talking to. "Ready?"

The four of them headed outside in the waning sunlight. Perfect. Just enough time to burn off their frustrations and work up an appetite. Those pies would *not* be scorned. At a fork in the cobblestone path, their groups split. Conrad cast her a final, unreadable glance. She put her nose in the air.

"Are we really hunting gold or are you planning to knock some sense into me?" Wyatt asked as soon as they were out of earshot of the others. "Because I already know I shouldn't have brought Lorelei. I just thought…I don't know. Con called me the other day, and I heard the frustration in his voice. I thought I'd help him out."

Her breath hitched. Conrad might wish he'd never moved in with her?

"Like an idiot," Wyatt continued, "I suspected he regretted moving here. I invited Lorelei to show him exactly what he's *not* missing. Didn't realize she'd pounce on him like a lioness on a gazelle. But more than that, being here...seeing Con with you, I realized I didn't have anything to worry about. Big bro was simply concerned about his lack of progress on your case. Seriously, the guy's a goner for you. He kept his attention on the kitchen the entire time you were cooking. At the table, he watched you. He doesn't want to be anywhere else, I can tell."

Comforting–troubling–words. "Has he told you about the Ladling curse?"

"He has." Wyatt reached out, clasped her hand and squeezed. "And if anyone can break that curse, it's Conrad."

Longing flooded her as they reached the gravesite of William King. "Yes. Well." Could he truly? Could anyone? "Thanks for looking out for him. You're a good brother."

He gave her a rueful grin. "He's the one who's always taken care of me. I'm just happy to help him any way I can. With that in mind, I'm gonna give you my best advice. Give him a chance. You'll never regret it." Before she could protest, he said, "So, what's our assignment?"

She cleared her throat to dislodge a sudden lump. "We're looking around, keeping the phrase *wailing milk* in mind."

They spent the next twenty minutes examining the massive headstone. Truly the biggest in the entire cemetery. They studied the carvings and noticed little nicks on the side that might or might not resemble tears. Hmm. She recalled the map she'd studied last night, and again, something niggled at the back of her mind.

*What am I missing? What, what?*

Footsteps sounded, Conrad and Lorelei approaching. The redhead appeared disappointed but resigned, while Conrad had shed layers of stress. Mission accomplished! Beau and

GENA SHOWALTER & JILL MONROE

Sora weren't far behind them. The pair had shed layers of stress as well. They weren't smiling, but they weren't uncomfortable anymore, either. Excellent.

"Anyone find anything?" Jane asked.

Negations rang out. But that was okay. She'd accomplished what she'd set out to do. "Who's ready to finish their meal and enjoy the reward of dessert?"

"Praise the Lord," Beau said. "I'm starved."

Conrad and Wyatt bumped forearms.

"I'm about to throw down on that turkey," Wyatt exclaimed.

The six of them returned to the cottage and their spots at the table. Suddenly, everyone was shoveling in food, passing bowls, talking, and laughing. The earlier agitation was gone. Cheddar prowled under the table, searching for scraps. Rolex hadn't abandoned his post above the fridge; he lay across the top, observing everything.

Jane caught Conrad's eye, and he smiled. She reclined in her seat, satisfaction oozing over her. You know, he and Beau were right. This might be the best holiday ever.

# CHAPTER EIGHT

A maid a-milking is worth her weight in gold. Or better yet,
love. A far more precious substance. But remember, a maid
isn't her best without her tools. Start with kindness, a sense
of humor and a zest for life.

–Lily Ladling's Holiday Advice for Ladies Cursed in Love

*J*ane hung Christmas lights in the Paradise
Ladling section of the Garden. She always decorated for her family first, then the permanent
guests. Otherwise her ancestors would stage a revolt; she just
knew it. Plus, she was eager to speak privately with Grandma
Lily.

Bonus: Jane didn't have to worry about Conrad overhear-
ing. He was gone when she woke up. Again, he'd left no note.
Had sent no text. Not that she was complaining. Or missing
him. Nope. She'd chosen her path. Now she had to live with
the consequences.

Mist plumed in front of her face as she exhaled. Even though golden sunshine bathed the land, the temperature had dropped ten degrees, bringing a crisp chill scented with pine and burning wood. Like most of the other sections in the cemetery, a hedgerow of southern wax myrtle cordoned off the area. She smiled at the bluish winter berries growing in clusters on each bush and remembered how Grandma Lily used to pluck them off to create aromatic candles.

Hmm, that might be a custom Jane should revive. All the necessary supplies were stored in the shed and who *wouldn't* want a candle made from berries found growing on the grounds of a cemetery? Cha-ching! Talk about the perfect money-making opportunity now that fresh bodies had stopped showing up on the property.

She crossed to her grandmother's familiar gray, coarse-grain marble headstone with carvings of lilies lining the sides and brushed off a few dried pine needles. Opal and Benjamin lived in this area as well, though the carvings on their headstones had been softened by time.

"You remember how we used to lament all those people who thought gold was buried somewhere on the grounds?" Jane began, pausing to adjust the angle of her snow cap and double check the top button of her coat. "Well, it turns out they may not have been too far off the mark. Just a few decades too late. I found great-grandfather Benjamin's old journal, and it looks like he found it. Guess that's why he ran off."

Grandma Lily didn't need to know the salacious details about his affair with Elise Dansing, and the possibility of a kinship with Tiffany Hotchkins, who could return to town any day. A sigh escaped, filling the air with mist. Maybe the holiday had injected a little hope into Jane's heart because she kind of wanted to try and make friends with the other woman. It might be nice to have another living relative. For both of them.

"Thank you for your letters." An ache of love and happiness tightened her chest. "I've been reading them. They mean the world to me. But I'm in a bit of a pickle, and I need more advice. I know Pops told you about the curse before you married him. Neither of you thought that curse would transfer to you the moment you took his last name. You thought the recipient had to be a Ladling by birth. But you were wrong. Pops ended up dying, wrecking you." She glanced at her grandfather's plot and winced. "Sorry, Pops, but it's true."

His headstone was the same northern Georgia marble as Lily's. A matching set for soulmates finally reunited.

"Sure, it seems like it was that faulty ticker of his that got him," Jane continued. "But we all know it was the curse, not his tendency to add mounds of bacon crumbles to every meal." She chewed on her bottom lip. "Did you ever regret wedding him?"

The wind kicked up a brown, dried leaf, and Jane dragged in a deep breath, steeling herself for what she was about to admit. "I may be, kind of, sort of falling for someone. Though I wish I wasn't! How can I circumvent the curse?"

Jane paused. Braced herself for a catastrophe to strike at even the tiniest admission of falling. Maybe a burst of spontaneous lightning that would deep fry the former agent. Or perhaps the Darien river beast coming out from the shadows, thinking to drag Conrad under a body of water, even though they weren't near an ocean.

But nothing.

Bolstered, she continued. "I mean, what if Conrad is right and all Ladling ladies lost their men because we cursed *ourselves*? We expected doom, therefore fear colored each of our thoughts and actions, paving the way to the very ending we sought to avoid. Stress *is* a leading factor of heart attacks, right? Need an example, look at Sheriff Moore. But honestly, I don't fit any of Conrad's qualifications for a girlfriend."

From the highest high to the lowest low. She wasn't unwaveringly kind, savagely honest, fiercely loyal, or lovingly vicious. Nor was she enchantingly naïve and bafflingly smart in the most illogical ways, with stunning confidence and odd insecurities in equal measure. *Right?*

Footsteps caught her attention, and she went still. Someone approached.

"We'll continue this conversation later," she whispered to her grandmother, then double-patted her headstone. As Grandma Lily used to say, one pat was never enough.

Rusty hinges released a shriek of protest as Fiona pushed past the iron gate positioned between two towering trees forever standing guard at the entrance of Paradise Ladling. She wore a lovely Christmas sweater that was black with bedazzled snowmen.

Overjoyed to see her friend, Jane hastened closer and hugged her tight. "Aren't you cold?"

Drawing back, Fee pretended to shiver. "Positively frosty. But wear a coat so no one gets to see this beauty? Not on your life."

Jane's eyes narrowed. "Oh really? How come you and Grandma Lily didn't understand such bulletproof logic when you insisted I wear Pops's old peacoat at Halloween, covering up my gorgeous princess costume?"

"That's the privilege of age," Fiona replied with a wink. "We get to be ridiculous knowing we're being ridiculous and not caring one whit."

Fair enough. "How was your first Thanksgiving with the sheriff and his family?" Jane asked with a smile.

"Oh, honey. I now know why my sweetie had a heart attack. Not a moment of levity and so many squabbles over the most trivial of things. Some tweet about potato salad nearly led to a knock down drag out rumble. And that was before Raymond's ex-wife arrived. How about you? How was *your* Thanksgiving?"

"Amazing, then terrible, then amazing again. By the end, it was so good I think I'm forever changed in the worst way." Jane gave her friend another hug. "The idea of ever spending a holiday without Conrad shreds me."

"Well, then. We both need a distraction, and I know just the thing," Fiona announced, tugging a skein of ruby red yarn from her bag.

Yes. The time had come to shift her focus off Conrad. "Knitting?"

"Better than that." The grandmother's infectious enthusiasm lifted Jane's spirits immediately. Until she heard her friend's next words. "Hon, it's time to put yourself back together again." The older woman drew out a pattern featuring a heart with a jagged line running along the center, separating it into two halves.

A broken heart, now mended.

Her spirits dropped once again, harder than a lead ball. "I'm not sure how knitting the heart will help."

"Jane Eleanor Ladling. Are you learning nothing from your Grandma Lily's letters? You need a reminder of what you're fighting for, and the finished heart will provide one. Really, what's a better risk than love?"

Stomach heavy, she shuffled a step back, as if she needed physical space from such a challenging question. "Maybe. But we're not just talking about me. I'll be putting Conrad's life in danger."

Fiona's head cocked to the side, and she lifted a brow. "If ever there was a man strong enough to break a curse, wouldn't it be Conrad?"

Exactly what Wyatt had said. And Beau. And Fiona.

Once again footsteps rang out, someone else approaching the area. Had Conrad returned at last? Anticipation engulfed her. And dread. Then, Conrad was there, sans Cheddar but with Beau.

The former agent looked incredible, as always, but he looked especially incredible bathed in morning light. Worn denim hugged his hips and molded to his powerful thighs. No matter what he wore, he always stole her breath.

Beau was a smoke show in his typical chief security officer outfit: black tactical pants and black polo with Peach State Security embroidered over his heart in, of course, peach. For some reason, he had rejected parading in the skintight faux leather pants Jane had found on the internet, because any thief or no-gooder would immediately surrender in the sight of such manliness. Beau had mumbled something about "impracticality" but c'mon. You had to dress for the job you wanted.

Both men grinned with so much satisfaction, they reminded her of Rolex after he munched on a grasshopper.

Fiona gave a little squeal and clapped her hands. "Is it time?"

"Oh, yeah," Beau said with a nod.

Jane's brow wrinkled, her gaze glued to Conrad. "Time for what?"

"It's a surprise," he told her. "But we need to leave now, or the show will start without us."

Show? They headed inside the cottage. While the others checked on the animals, Jane fetched her purse and a stunning fascinator hat with an array of bows. After blowing goodbye kisses to Rolex and Cheddar, she made her way to a shiny black SUV with all the bells and whistles. Sheriff Moore's maybe? A retirement gift to himself? Fiona must have driven it over.

Except, Conrad possessed the keys. He helped Jane into

the passenger seat, ever the gentleman, and climbed behind the wheel, with Fiona and Beau in back. Everything smelled brand new. Looked it, too.

"Whose car is this?" she asked.

"Mine," Conrad told her. "I sold Stella and picked up Jel this morning. Wanted more space to haul...things."

What! He'd sold his precious? To haul things? What things? But, but. Why? He'd loved that car. "What kind of name is Jel, anyway?"

Fiona tapped the back of her seat, and Jane twisted around to look at her.

*Your initials*, the other woman mouthed.

Oh.

*Oh.*

Butterflies took flight in her stomach. "It's, um, lovely."

As they maneuvered along the roads, Beau and Fiona whispered together, and Conrad explained the vehicle's every safety feature with the pride of a father to Jane, giving her a reprieve from the world-rocking realization. And honestly, crash prevention had never been so alluring. Or confusing. Seriously, what was he expecting to haul? Fine china?

"Who knew you'd geek out over automatic braking?" she said with a little laugh. "Now tell me about my surprise right this second or feel my wrath!"

His soft chuckle resounded between them. "I'm feeling daring today. I'm gonna risk it."

She winced at him. "Oh, Conrad. That mistake is gonna cost you dearly."

"Will you show me mercy if I give you a hint?"

"I'll consider the possibility of thinking about it."

"Fair enough." He stopped at the front gate of the Palisades, the wealthiest neighborhood in town. Where the mansions resided. A place Jane had visited often during each of her murder investigations. For the first time, the gate was manned by a guard.

As soon as Conrad flashed his badge, the guard pressed a button to the entrance. Tiffany Hotchkins lived one street over. Were they headed there? Had she returned?

Hmm. Conrad didn't turn onto her street. Instead, he kept advancing forward. "We're all about to witness something on each of our bucket lists."

Ohhhh. How intriguing. What did she want that Conrad, Fiona and Beau also wanted? "A top-of-the-line shelter for abandoned and stray pets, where animals live in bedrooms of their own instead of cages? A restaurant where Fiona serves blueberry pancakes upon request, and she can never ever say no? A hat museum with the option to rent the displays if you purchase a frequent visitor pass?"

"Better," Conrad vowed. He parked in front of a large, sprawling Mediterranean estate with arched stonework windows and three balconies. A delightful umber-tiled roof completed, a towering rotunda.

Jane had a direct view of the one-of-a-kind wooden front door. Unable to contain her excitement, she shifted in her seat. Better than the shelter? Impossible!

"That," her ex said, pointing to the brownstone, "is Devin Hagger's home."

Oookay. "Go on."

"They're coming, they're coming," Fiona cried.

A vehicle pulled into the driveway. Then another and another. A dark sedan and two cop cars with their lights flashing. No sirens blared, though. Because the drivers didn't want to offend the residents of the expensive neighborhood?

Her eyes widened as a woman she'd met on numerous occasions emerged from the sedan. Special Agent Karen Hightower. Uniformed police officers hastened to flank her sides. The group approached the front door and knocked with firm persistence. When Hagger opened, one of the uniformed officers stepped forward. While Jane couldn't hear them, she imagined the imposing lawyer demanded a warrant before anyone entered his home.

Only, they didn't enter. What in heaven's name—Panic wiped away the man's usual haughty expression as he wrenched back. The officer caught him by one shoulder and spun him around, then cuffed his wrists together.

"He's being arrested?" Jane gasped out.

"He is. The charge is attempted murder. Among other things." Conrad smiled with cold satisfaction, and it was as chilling as it was beautiful. "He paid the mechanic to rig your hearse. We found proof of a money transfer between the mechanic and one of Hagger's former clients. Hagger used evidence he'd uncovered during a former investigation to blackmail the client into doing it. That client kept records of everything."

Hagger was the one who'd wanted Jane dead? Wow, wow, wow. They'd had their spats during the last investigation, when she'd accused him of murdering his partner, but ending her life had been his solution?

No doubt he'd be out on bail before he was tossed into a cell and the key melted, trapping him forever. Or something like that. But whatever went down, he had no reason to come after Jane again. The Hearse Gone Wild case was officially over. So why wasn't she bouncing with joy?

"He must really hate me," she said softly.

Her amazing ex reached over to take her hand, offering comfort. His warmth supplied just that. "He was afraid of you. At the time, you were digging into Tony's activities, which would have led you to Hagger's activities. He had a lot to hide. Blackmails. Briberies. Pyramid schemes. I only wish I could have been the one to take him in."

Yes, she heard the relish in his tone. "Who realized the truth?"

"I did." He gave her a sheepish grin. "I applied the things I've learned at the Jane Ladling School of Solving Mysteries and Other Cool Stuff."

"He isn't kidding," Beau piped up. "He had me going down some seriously wild rabbit holes online."

"I'll require a full outline later," she replied, too stunned to insist upon it now.

Beau answered her with a salute.

"Whatever we learned, I passed along to Hightower." Conrad gave her hand another squeeze before drawing away. Or trying to. Jane had a death grip on him. Her cheeks heated as she realized it. In a scramble, she released him. "A forensic team found the smoking gun. I've been expecting this moment for days."

Pumping her fist toward the roof of the SUV, Fiona called, "Justice is served on ice!"

"I should send his receptionist another batch of my famous butter pecan cupcakes." A way of saying *sorry your boss is such a tool and you are out of a job.*

"The ones with the maple glaze?" Fiona asked with interest.

"Ladies, you're going to miss the best part," Conrad said as a police officer dragged a defiant Devin Hagger down the walkway and stuffed him into the back of the squad car.

Jane had been in the back of one of those vehicles earlier this year, and the posh attorney was in for a rude awakening after the cushy surroundings of his opulent home.

"Thank you," she said to everyone in the SUV as the police car containing her would-be killer pulled away. These people had refused to give up; they'd done everything in their power to protect her. Especially Conrad. The man had moved into her home for heaven's sake. There was no stopping the flood of tender emotion swamping her. "I love you all so much."

The second the words registered, she sucked in a breath. The others went quiet. Oh...darn, darn, darn. Drats! Crap! Crappity crap crap! Jane met Conrad's stunned gaze.

What had she done? Could she have dared...had she... had she just invited love into her life?

# CHAPTER NINE

Get to dancing, lady! There's nothing like celebrating
Christmas in the arms of a man who adores you. And
nothing draws said man nearer than a flirty tango.

–Lily Ladling's Holiday Advice for Ladies Cursed in Love

*J*ane had big plans today. Namely, a trip to the
Yellow Brick Abode Library. Always a fun experience. Walking through those sliding glass
doors never failed to ramp up her anticipation and fill her
head with possibilities. Had been that way since Grandma
Lily first accompanied her for story time with Miss Nancy.
Today's quest–looking over the old town maps of the cemetery. The reference section offered papers, flyers and books
unavailable online, as well as older tomes donated by local
residents. She just might hit pay dirt.

But that visit had to wait until she looked at a house and
possibly lost her roommate for good.

Mouth going dry, Jane entered the empty home with Conrad and his realtor, Buddy Horn. Buddy wore a red and black herringbone tie probably purchased brand new in 1973. He was a little taller than her and reed thin, with kind eyes and a mischievous smile. An old-fashioned gentleman rake. The scent of cigarette smoke clung to him. No wedding ring.

"Tons of potential, right? These craftsman bungalows in the Bedrock neighborhood don't come up often," Buddy said, performing a slow spin with his arms spread. A breathtaking stained-glass window ensured he remained bathed in colorful sunlight, dust motes glittering all around him. "I think it's charming, but my opinion isn't the one that matters. Why don't I leave you two love birds alone while you check everything out? I'll be on the porch if you need me."

"Good idea," Conrad replied, surprising her. He didn't correct the man's "love birds" comment, but then, neither did she.

Hinges squeaked as Buddy exited the home. Jane busied herself with a walk around the living room, her kitten heels tapping against the scratched and water-stained hardwood floor.

She crouched to tap on a couple of the planks. "These will need to be sanded and refinished, but the bones are good. And that will need to be repainted," she said, pointing to the chipped wainscoting in the dining area. She could already picture the table, covered with food and surrounded by friends, family and children. Grandma Lily's cast-iron, five-tier candelabra as centerpiece.

No. Not Grandma Lily's anything. Conrad's wife would choose something, perhaps an antique memento from her own family. Jane mashed her lips together and crossed toward the giant bay window overlooking the yard.

GENA SHOWALTER & JILL MONROE

As she pretended to study the seal along the frame, a thousand thoughts raced through her mind. Most revolved around Conrad and their relationship. Well, not a relationship at the moment, but still a friendship. Except...she'd practically shouted her love. Sure, she'd made the unintended declaration to a group of people, but what had it meant?

It meant she'd opened a door, that's what. To more than just friendship. To sharing part of her life with Conrad. To a future.

No, she hadn't just opened a door, she'd flung the thing off its hinges, turned on the porch light and rolled out a welcome mat.

Her hands grew clammy as a cold sweat broke out along the back of her neck. Though she'd spoken of friendship, only friendship, she couldn't negate the words. The damage was already done. Did that mean she was soon to lose Conrad? Perhaps he'd find a new job somewhere else in a month. Maybe, in a year, he would meet his dream woman in Atlanta and decide to return to the city. Maybe it would happen in a decade. Did it really matter if the curse was real or self-inflicted? Jane believed it; he was right about that. Meaning, the end result was the same. Loss.

How did someone go about changing their whole belief system? Forgetting a lifetime of expectation in favor of hope for something better?

What she suddenly knew beyond any doubt? The road she currently traveled with Conrad wasn't the right one. Be it fate, destiny or curse, and she was to lose him regardless, why not fight for something better while she had the chance?

Maybe Wyatt and Fiona were right. What if Conrad *could* break the curse? Why not give *him* a chance? You missed a hundred percent of the shots you didn't take.

Something cracked inside her. Just a smidge, but enough. The very hope she'd lamented only moments ago bloomed through the new opening. An optimism so rare, Jane almost didn't recognize it.

Here it was, her answer. Taking a chance on him. Because he was worth it. More than worth it. Of course, marriage would never be an option. No way she'd risk his life on top of everything else. But dating him? Enjoying him until he broke the curse...or not? Yes, yes, a thousand times yes. She'd been a fool to break things off with him.

"What do you think so far?" Conrad asked, pulling her from her thoughts.

She rotated to face him, peering up at his handsome face and beaming.

He stilled, only the muscles in his throat seeming to work. "Whatever I did to deserve that smile, tell me so I can do it again."

"The house is kind of perfect," she told him with conviction. "Buddy's right. Character is seeping from the built-in bookcases to the window seat. There's a ton of potential." Plus, Conrad wouldn't live too far from the Garden. "And you do like to fix things."

With his lopsided smile in place, he took her hand. "Come on. Let's see the rest."

They strolled up the stairs, finding three bedrooms on the second floor. Their fingers remained twined, neither letting go. She didn't let herself ponder what that could mean on his behalf. Not yet.

"When I was a little boy in foster care," he said, the gentleness of his tone surprising her as much as his willingness to initiate a conversation about his past, "I used to lay in bed and tell myself I'd live in a house of my own one day, and no one would be able to take it away from me."

A lump clogged her throat. This man might be as tough as nails, but he was as sweet as cotton candy too. "You deserve the best life, Conrad. You really do."

He squeezed her hand. "So do you, Jane."

She struggled to focus as they returned downstairs. But focus she did. He brought her here to get her honest opinion, so she would give it. "The layout of the kitchen reminds me of the cottage," she told him the lump dissolved. "It's open and flows into the rest of the house with just the right amount of old-world charm. I love it." Dang it! There she went, slinging the L word around all willy-nilly again.

In a show of mercy, he stayed silent today just as he'd stayed quiet yesterday. The tension evaporated from her, deflating her shoulders.

"Did I hear someone singing praises?" Buddy popped back into the room, a bright smile on his face. "There's a study attached to the master bedroom, which you could also use as a, ahem, nursery. And Mr. Ryan, did you say you had a dog?"

"The perfect little corgi," Jane answered, eager to get past talk of babies and nurseries.

"The backyard is already fenced for your little guy," Buddy pointed out. "Well, are you ready to render the final verdict?"

Still Conrad maintained a steady hold on her. The pull between them never lessened.

She tilted her head back, peering up at him through the shield of her lashes. "It's the kind of home I would buy for myself," she admitted softly, "if I didn't adore living at the cemetery, of course."

"Did you say cemetery?" Buddy piped up.

"Then this is it," Conrad said, ignoring the realtor. His amber eyes hooded as his warm breath fanned her face. "The house I'm buying."

The air thickened, her inhalations instantly quickening. Maybe her hope had given her courage. Or maybe seeing him embrace the future spurred her to embrace hers. Feeling brave, she rasped, "Do you want to date me again, Conrad?"

One corner of his mouth lifted. "Sweetheart, I never wanted to stop."

"Oh, dang." From the corner of her eye, she saw Buddy slap his knee. "Did I just repair a broken relationship?"

Jane ignored him, too caught up in Conrad to care about anything else. "You want to date me even though I don't fit your qualifications?" Though, granted, she *was* a little bit amazing. The kind of person she wanted as a friend. Someone with her priorities straight. Cats, hats and family. Not necessarily in that order...not all the time. And, honestly, she was good at being modest. Great, even. And she *could* whip up a feast just because, using only the ingredients she had on hand.

Could she turn his heartache and anguish into tools?

His smile grew. "Jane, you *are* the qualifications."

Sniffling sounds came from Buddy. "That is beautiful."

Joy stirred deep in her chest, as if awakening from a long-time slumber. "You aren't over me?" she asked, running her free palm up Conrad's chest to toy with the ends of his hair.

He released her hand, but only to cup her jawline. "Not in the slightest." His thumbs caressed the rise of her cheeks. "And you aren't over me." A statement, not a question.

"No," she admitted. "Conrad Ryan, will you go on a date with me?"

"Jane Ladling, I will go on *all* the dates with you."

Buddy dabbed at his eyes.

Jane's internal fluttering worsened. "Rolex and Cheddar are going to be over the moon." As she peered up at her inspector detective special agent, excited and nervous, an idea blossomed inside her mind like the most beautiful rose, if she did say so herself. She'd put him through a lot, and even if whatever they started tomorrow lasted only a short time, he deserved a grand gesture. "Tomorrow night. Seven p.m. The cottage, just the two of us. Wear your black suit with a black tie. Bring flowers."

Conrad's slow smile left her heart fluttering. "It's a date."

JANE SPLIT from Conrad as soon as they left the house and headed for the library. She forced the date to the back of her mind as she parked in the lot. She had business to attend. Wait. Was that Tiffany Hotchkins's bright red sports car?

Well, well, well. The widow had indeed returned. Somewhere inside, the prickly brunette strolled along the aisles of the noble building.

To postpone this expedition or not?

Not. Jane wore her Big Girl badge today. She'd asked a man on a date, and she was soon to solve the Case of the Great Grand Cheater and His Missing Heart of Gold. Face Tiffany? No problem.

Head high, Jane strode across the tree-lined sidewalk. Large plastic bulbs already hung from the limbs. The library was located next door to the Gold Rush Museum, a former county courthouse constructed to be imposing. Meanwhile, the library's homestyle curb appeal invited visitors inside.

She slipped through the doors, passing beneath the banner proclaiming: *Books, Stories and Adventures, oh my!*

On her way to the map case, Jane passed by the nonfiction section dedicated to ciphers and code breaking and drew up short. Hey! She'd found Tiffany already. The widow stood alongside her best friend, the infamous Abigail Waynes-Kirkland. Their dark heads were bent over a book. Both wore their hair in tight top buns and sported heavy coats because the library always attempted to freeze patrons out, even in winter.

They were interested in codes and code breaking huh? Suspicions flared in an instant. They'd amped up their search for gold, hadn't they? She swallowed a groan. Maybe becoming friends was a pipe dream. Hoping not to be noticed, Jane inched closer to catch as much of their conversation as possible. Probably not a technique listed in Conrad Ryan's investigative methods, but for sure it belonged in the procedures and practices manual she was now considering writing.

"Mule easel could only be a cipher," Tiffany muttered. "It's too weird."

So. Benjamin's phrases must have been in his letters to Elise. And yet, this pair hadn't yet figured out the anagram angle. *Several steps behind me.* The coil of tension between her shoulder blades eased.

"Sunken ice naps could mean diamonds are buried in her cemetery. We should do some digging. I still have my trusty shovel," Abigail said, and they both snickered.

Jane curled her hands into fists. Okay, done listening. Time to start promising. Stalking forward, she announced, "If I catch you attempting to unearth a grave at the Garden, I will make sure you're eating Christmas dinner in jail!"

Both women gasped; they glanced up in unison. Tiffany slammed the book closed. Jane pounced, snatching the tome before the widow realized her intentions, and clutched it to her chest. With a fiery glare, she dared anyone to try and take it from her.

Tiffany lifted her chin, bristling with defiance. "If we're related, half of the gold belongs to me."

"First of all, the gold is gone," Jane informed her. "Benjamin vanished with it the very night he believed he'd deciphered the code." Maybe. Probably.

Abigail radiated pure smugness. "That's what you think."

Tiffany elbowed her friend, the tried and true "you said too much" gesture. She refocused squarely on Jane. "Look. I found Elise's letters to Benjamin mixed in with his letters to her. She wrote that her husband knew about her affair, and he was out for Benjamin's blood. And obviously, great grand-daddy succeeded, because how else would Elise get her own letters back?"

So...what? Tiffany's ancestor murdered Jane's ancestor before he got his hands on the gold? Like, great Grandpa Dansing had snatched great Grandpa Ladling straight from the caretaker's office as he composed his final entry in his own journal? Then, in the aftermath, Dansing found the stash of letters and took them to shame his wife—or hide her shame?

Hmm. A good story, but something didn't sit right. Jane's gut said, *Keep digging.*

"Or," she said, "Elise planned to kill Benjamin so she framed her husband, then stole the letters so that no one would ever learn her secret."

The widow and her friend humphed. "Either way, there could be a stash of gold on your property," Tiffany said. "Or rather, *our* property."

Abigail smirked again. "As a soon-to-be co-owner, Tiff will have every right to do whatever she wants to the place, whenever she wants."

"Does she want half the bills, too?" Jane snapped. Wait. Wait, wait, wait. *Oh my goodness!* Her mouth floundered open and closed, words dying in her throat. A thought hit her like a wrecking ball, and she stumbled back. No. No, no, no. It couldn't be verified yet. But...

The possibility seemed more and more likely.

She swallowed a groan. Tiffany Hotchkins *must* be a Ladling. Look at her luck with men. She had loved her husband…and he'd died. She later thought she'd found the true love of her life…and she'd lost him when he'd turned out to be a heartless murderer.

Who needed a DNA test with proof this solid? *She's cursed.*

*Just like me.* And Jane had just asked Conrad on a date. Cold fingers of fear crept up her spine, closing around her mind. But she shook her head, hard. No. No! She wasn't doing this again. She wasn't giving in to the dreaded "what if."

They weren't forever. She knew and accepted that. But they were right now, and that was good enough.

*But when has good enough ever been, well, good enough?*

"Share the gold, or lose half the Garden," Tiffany grated. "I'm not afraid to sue. And the cemetery *is* an ancestral estate, is it not?"

Finally, Jane found her voice. Threaten her home? Big mistake. If the other woman pushed any harder, the gloves would came off, and the brass knuckles would come on. Metaphorically speaking, of course. In fact, she almost—almost!—used Conrad's upcoming sheriffship to her advantage. Because guaranteed he would win. That wasn't even a question. No one had a better record or skill set. Which gave her an idea for the perfect Christmas gift for him. Oh! He was going to love it.

*Focus.* "The Garden is an ancestral estate, yes," she allowed with a stiff tone. "There was a will naming me as the beneficiary, and inheritance rights always follow the will. Meaning your case has no legs. Why do you want the gold? If there is even a single nugget left. You're already rich."

Red circles painted Tiffany's cheeks, and another realization hit Jane.

Her eyes widened. "You're broke. Your murderous fiancé drained your bank accounts before his capture, didn't he?"

Theft had been his specialty, after all. A product of his bottomless greed, and the reason he'd killed to hide his activities.

The red circles expanded, covering more ground.

Sympathy welled, but still Jane said, "Why don't you have your lawyer call mine?" In other words, no one would be calling anyone about anything. Tiffany probably couldn't afford to hire a lawyer at this point.

The widow and her friend floundered for a response.

Done with the conversation, Jane pivoted and headed for the reference section, exactly as planned. One thing had become crystal clear. She must solve the mystery of Benjamin's treasure now, now, now. No more delays or distractions.

Well, other than her date.

# CHAPTER TEN

Do you ever wonder why lords start a-leaping? I think it's because they've found the greatest gift of all—love! No matter how bad things appear, love never fails, Jane. Remember that.

–Lily Ladling's Holiday Advice for Ladies Cursed in Love

*Knock, knock.* The hard double rap sounded at Jane's bedroom door, and she sucked air between her teeth. Conrad!

"He's here," she whispered to Rolex. In a matter of seconds, their date would begin. She forced any lingering thoughts of maps and newspaper articles and journal entries from her mind. Almost. She'd come home with pictures of everything she'd studied at the library, but so far she'd learned nothing new. And yet, the map remained a niggle she couldn't shake.

Her furry beast of love dropped the ornament he'd been

carrying between his teeth, hopped on the bed and lifted his leg to lick his belly. Oh, how precious! He wanted to look his best, too.

Tremors sped through Jane's limbs as she slid her gaze to the clock on her nightstand. 6:51 p.m.. The tremors worsened. Conrad had arrived nine minutes before she'd expected him. Impatient to see her? Even early, though, his timing couldn't have been better. She'd just finished crocheting both parts of the broken heart Fiona had given her, keeping her hands busy as she considered all things gold and Garden. Now she had only to sew the pieces together, creating the perfect metaphor for mending her own heart.

Palms damp, Jane smoothed the sides of her dress. A black, curve-hugging number she'd paired with a 1930's mourning hat. A shoulder length ebony veil cascaded over the wide brim. She'd even gone the extra mile and strapped on high heels.

One last glance at her hair—she'd pinned the sides beneath the hat, the rest free-flowing and curling at the ends. Not a strand out of place. Excellent. She settled a wool wrap around her shoulders, drew in a deep breath, and opened the door to her...boyfriend.

At the sight of him, her heart swelled and her skin warmed. Oh, wow, he looked good. Beyond good. Glorious! He hadn't shaved this morning, and a thicker shadow covered his strong jaw. The dark suit fit him like perfection itself. He'd gone with a black collared shirt and a silk tie. His Oxfords gleamed. Freshly polished? In his hands waited a bouquet of jet-black roses.

"Jane." His amber gaze slid over her and the corners of his mouth lifted with delight. "You are exquisite."

At the base of her throat, her pulse jumped. "And you are...mine," she rasped. *For now.*

His smile deepened. "The best of all my features." He

offered her the flowers, and she blushed with pleasure as she accepted the sweet-smelling blooms. Their inky color made her think he suspected the activity she had planned.

She clutched the bouquet close and extended her free arm. "Shall we?"

"We shall." As he twined his fingers through hers, he asked, "Our destination?"

"Valley of the Dolls." A section of the Garden without bodies, thanks to a maze of interlocking tree roots. There, she had hosted funerals for her deceased toys, living her childhood dream of becoming a funeral director. Ah. Such sweet memories.

As Conrad led her downstairs, Rolex darted past them. Probably on the hunt for Cheddar, ready for a new staring contest.

Speaking of... "Where's the sweetest dog on the planet?"

"He's spending the night with Uncle Beau."

They exited the house through the back door, entering the chill of the night. This morning, she'd created a path of colorful LED globes to the Valley of the Dolls. The scenic route. They went through Angel Wing, the Reflection Center, passed the headstone of the resident dog, Muffin, through Autumn Grove, Pleasant Green, and Serenity Rose.

"The owner of the house accepted my offer," Conrad said. "We sign papers the week after Christmas."

"Oh, that's so wonderful. Congratulations. You are going to be so happy there."

"Agreed." They entered Paradise Ladling, where Conrad paused. Twinkle lights glowed from trees. Simple grapevine wreaths topped with sprigs of pine decorated each gravestone. Pinecones coated in peanut butter and dipped in birdseed kept the Garden's wildlife happy and fed.

He squeezed her hand, wonder etched in his expression as he looked around. "I've never been in this section at night.

It's enchanting. And that is not a word I ever thought to use, but no other description fits."

This particular man didn't brush off her admittedly odd, well, oddities; no, he encouraged them.

*Someone who appreciates her quirks.* His very words after Jane had asked him to describe his ideal woman.

A dreamy sigh left her, and she rested her head on his shoulder. How she loved breathing in his incredible scent. "Come on," she said. "The ceremony is about to start. We just need to follow the paper lanterns." Nighttime funerals weren't the norm, but occasionally a family had asked for an evening vigil; she always prepared the Garden with dozens of paper lanterns, sand and LED candles.

Brows furrowed, he strode forward, keeping her tucked into his side as they entered the Valley of the Dolls. "Ceremony?"

"Mmm mmm." So he actually had no clue about her plans. How wonderful! The less he knew, the better the surprise.

Jane's heart leaped as she spotted the magnolia tree which had offered such amazing and terrible advice as she'd struggled under the influence of jimsonweed. Long story involving the accidental ingestion of poison.

The tree's words haunted her. *You're regret. Miss Regret Cursed the Fourth.*

She reached up and smoothed her finger over one of the still green leaves. "Not regret any longer," she mumbled. From this day forward, she'd be Miss Joy, uh, Blessed the First. Or something like that. She would workshop the name.

"What did you say?" Conrad asked.

She smiled up at him. "Someday I'll tell you all about the conversation I had with this very magnolia after accidentally consuming that thorn apple seed."

His shoulders shook with laughter. "I still have some of your voicemails saved on my phone."

What! Jane paused to plant her hands on her hips. "Sir, I insist you delete those immediately."

He dropped a kiss on the tip of her nose. "But you were so adorable."

Well…how was she supposed to argue with that? "Though you don't deserve it," she said, dragging out her phone and pressing play, "we shall begin." A soft, instrumental melody filled the air. Then she drew him to a small "gravesite" she'd arranged earlier. A wooden headstone rose from a mound of dirt, bearing the words *Conrad and Jane's Breakup*.

He barked out a laugh. "I thought I'd get a tour, but you're hosting a funeral."

Using her most soothing tone, she said, "Well, I'm so sorry for your loss, Officer Detective Inspector Special Agent Future Sheriff Ryan. The time has come to acknowledge the passing of our breakup." Taking her performance to the next level, she patted his shoulder in a gesture of faux comfort.

His amber eyes twinkled in the moonlight. "I've been over it. Actually, I never acknowledged it in the first place."

"Yes. Well. Denial is a stage of grief. And now it's time for the reading." Jane cleared her throat as she pulled a piece of paper from a coat pocket. "It's often said that for every woman with a broken heart, there is a man who knows how to weld."

His warm chuckle thrilled her. "I do know how to weld. Consider your heart whole with me."

Jane lifted a finger in mock sternness to show that now was not the time for an interruption. "In closing, some breakups are meant for makeups. And that concludes our service for the evening. Refreshments will be served in the cottage, but stay here as long as you need, alright? Silently reflect on the good times. Say a few words. Whatever feels right. There's nowhere else I'd rather be than right here with you. I'll help you through this difficult time however I can."

Laughing again, he swooped down to give her a swift kiss on the lips. Her heartbeat kicked into overdrive. She offered him the bundle of roses he'd given her, and he accepted.

He crouched before the gravestone. "I can't say I ever liked you." He laid the flowers over the dirt mound one by one. "You challenged me, humbled me, and forced me to be patient. I now know the meaning of long-suffering. And yes, I rejoiced as you breathed your last breath. But in the end, you crushed and burned, gifting me with my great happiness."

Flutters here, and flutters there. Flutters everywhere.

When he straightened, he slid his arm around Jane's waist once more, as if he couldn't bear to be apart from her too long. "I think my favorite part of our breakup was the moment I realized you had switched into matchmaker mode. I got to plead my case before the judge, before I realized my trial had even started."

Smiling and blushing in unison, she leaned her head on his shoulder. "Want to know what tipped the scales in your favor?"

"Only more than anything," he admitted.

"It's simple, really. You are you."

His grip on her tightened. He kissed the top of her head. "Your turn to have some fun. Let's go to the mausoleum and solve that mystery already. I know you want to. And I've been thinking about that map. There's something about it…"

"Yes! The map," she said, two thousand percent on board. "I agree there's something there. Let's go."

"Along the way, you can tell me all about your run-in with Tiffany Hotchkins."

Her jaw slackened. "How did you know? I never told you."

He gave her one of her favorite looks: *Sweetheart, please. Your man has ways.*

As he escorted her along the path, her mind whirled. No

doubt he'd heard in one of two ways. "Either gossip spread to Fiona's wellness center, and she let you know, or you're logging too many hours on the Headliner. Considering my darling Fiona is practically living with Sheriff Moore now, I'm going with the Headliner. Final answer." The message board allowed residents of Aurelian Hills to stay up to date on all the recent happenings.

"I like to keep track of certain topics," he said with an unashamed shrug.

This man. Oh, this man. "So the run-in with Tiffany. She's desperate, even suggesting part of this land belongs to her, but I set her straight. Besides, you know the golden rule. Whoever has gold, rules."

"You'll be the one to find it, I have no doubts."

"You aren't wrong." She fluffed her hair. "But when you become sheriff, I expect you to arrest Tiffany Hotchkins and Abigail Waynes-Kirkland immediately. As my boyfriend, it's practically your sworn duty. In fact, it should be your first act upon taking office. Charge them with inciting a riot in my head. And kidnapping my calm!"

He thought for a moment, then shrugged. "Sounds fair."

"We *must* solve the mystery before they do. Bragging rights, the most important prize of all, are at stake."

"And possibly gold."

"Yes, that too. I'm kicking myself for even considering trying to become Tiffany's friend."

"I predict you'll be best friends in the coming months."

Ha! He'd see. They reached the mausoleum, where silvery moonlight glistened from the aged stones. Bright Christmas bulbs glowed, spotlighting the tinsel Jane and Fiona had hung on the pine trees.

Inside the elaborate structure, Conrad and Jane paused to examine the mural. For some reason, Paradise Ladling snagged her attention. She had searched Silas Ladling's headstone and grave in about every way possible. Heck, she and Beau had even dug it up during the first murder investigation. Nothing. And yet…that niggling in the back of her mind wouldn't let up. But what was she missing?

She circled Silas's gravesite with her finger, then recalled the circles Benjamin had drawn all over the list. Wait. Circles. She moved to William King's gravesite and circled it with her finger, too.

Was this location different from the maps she presented to guests?

"The artist did exceptional work," Conrad said. "Highly detailed."

Information spilled from her by route. "That's because of Evangeline Ladling, the oldest daughter of Silas. She was the original artist of the family, known for throwing lavish parties in her old age and stealing the heart of every suitor in town during her younger years. She's the reason we were cursed, you know. Anyway. Other artistically inclined Ladlings have added details to the map throughout the years." She might have told him that already. This time, the tidbit caught her attention. Changes…circles. Circles, changes.

"Lavish parties and stealing hearts, hmm? Did she happen to have long dark hair and big blue eyes full of possibilities?"

Jane's blush returned. "If we were texting this conversation, I would so message you L.O.L. right now."

"Lots of love?" he asked with a teasing tone. Her blush burned hotter, and he barked out a full blown laugh. "Too soon? You're the one shouting it in cars."

Her lips parted to protest, but…protest what? His contagious amusement?

The cruel tormentor showed a smidgen of mercy and drew an air circle around a monument. "If I'm looking at this correctly, this is in Paradise Ladling, yes?"

"Yes," she verified. Changes, circles.

"The ancestor who hid the gold probably put it in a section reserved for family. Or at least a portion of it. Fewer disturbances, higher level of control."

"Good thinking." She returned to the image depicting Silas's gravesite, joining Conrad at the wall. They automatically drew together, and the most delicious contentment washed over her.

"Hmm," he said, staring intently at the map.

"What else are you theorizing?" she asked, nudging her shoulder against his arm.

"I don't know yet," he replied. "But there's definitely something here..." He wound his arm around her waist, cupping her hip, and she felt her blush return. He wasn't just talking about clues in the mausoleum. And to think, she'd wasted so much time pushing him away, avoiding feelings.

Jane leaned her head against Conrad's shoulder and looked from Silas to William to Sueann Pickens.

Circles, changes.

She breathed in her companion's scent. Yes, there was definitely something here.

# CHAPTER ELEVEN

Legend says a piper gets to pipping when two hearts become one. Or something like that. Wouldn't you like to hear some music, Jay Bird?

–Lily Ladling's Holiday Advice for Ladies Cursed in Love

*A*s one day after another passed, Tiffany and Abigail never snuck onto cemetery grounds with shovels. Strange, considering the widow's dire financial straits. According to the Headliner, she'd put the mansion up for sale and sought a job overseeing events at the Manor on Prospect, the fanciest hotel in town.

According to sources, rumors also claimed a couple of lawsuits were headed her way, thanks to her husband, who might have done more than use his exam rooms as a rotating harem. Apparently, Tiffany's lawyer—the widow did have one, after all—had advised her to keep her nose clean. Being arrested for trespassing on Jane's property certainly wouldn't classify as walking the straight and narrow.

Whatever the reason for the reprieve, Jane was grateful. But. Thanks to holiday prep, she'd gotten no further in her own investigation. Now, with the arrival of Christmas Eve, she had even more to do. At least she knew deep down she finally hovered at the cusp of a solve. It felt as if every possibility she'd ever entertained filled a mental bottle and any upcoming ideas would drip inside and force an overflow. *So close I can taste it!*

Humming under her breath, she transferred fresh baked cookies from the pan to a serving bowl. Each sweet treat bore one of five shapes, with frosting to match. There was a gingerbread man, a Christmas tree, a wreath, a star and a holly leaf. Any moment, her guests would begin arriving at the Garden. Her inner circle.

With such a beloved group of friends, she'd thought, *Why not revive a Ladling tradition?* Something else she'd let slip after her grandmother's death. She'd even selected a special dress for the occasion—a red and black tartan print, asymmetrically gathered at the waist with a sprig of holly at the collar.

Rolex watched her from the table, curled up inside his favorite spot, the centerpiece bowl.

"I'm gonna have to double up on ab days, but your cooking is worth it," Conrad said, stepping up behind her. His delectable warmth enveloped her.

Being his girlfriend again came with amazing perks. "Don't be silly. These are maple cookies. Maple. Maple syrup comes from trees, which means these cookies are plant based."

Chuckling, he nuzzled his cheek against hers. "In that case..." He pilfered two cookies before dancing out of reach, already biting into one, ensuring she couldn't snatch it back.

His golden irises glittered before his lids briefly slid shut. "How do you bring Heaven to Earth with flour, eggs and sugar?"

With his attention diverted, she gave him the I'm-the-girlfriend-so-I-get-to head-to-toe examination. Dang, he looked good in jeans, boots and a smile aimed right at her. And double dang, she wanted to answer his question with the word *love*. The secret ingredient Grandma Lily used. But nope. Not going there. "I only tell my recipes to good boys who don't steal cookies meant for guests."

Unrepentant, he finished off said cookies. "Exactly what is this tradition we're doing tonight?"

"I'll explain after our guests arrive."

Something she'd said must have thrilled him because he grinned with pure mischievousness before nodding. "Deal. Now how about another cookie?"

The sound of scrambling paws reached her ears, and she laughed. Cheddar zoomed into the kitchen with his tail wagging, as if expecting a cookie of his own.

Rolex reached out an arm, stretching and baring his claws. Specks of blue glitter sparkled between two paw pads. Obviously, the darling boy had been playing with the Christmas tree ornaments again.

"Mommy and Da—her boyfriend have friends arriving shortly, baby. You be good, and I'll give you extra treats." Flushing with mortification from head to toe at her slip, she blew the furry love of her life a kiss. Had she really almost referred to Conrad as the cat's father?

The feline blinked at her, and she thought the gesture might mean *how dare you attempt to withhold my due.*

Jane collected the bowl of cookies. With Conrad and Cheddar, she made her way to the living room. As expected, the others arrived, everyone hugging everyone else. Fiona and the sheriff. Beau. Trick, Holden and Isaac.

Trick swiped a cookie and popped it into his mouth. A groan left him as he chewed. "I swear your cooking makes my IQ drop," he told her as soon as he swallowed. "One bite, and I can think of nothing but getting more. Good thing I'm okay with just being pretty." He swiped two other treats.

"Save some for the rest of us." Isaac, with his dark skin and glorious eyes, elbowed Trick aside to snag three cookies. Holden, who had always reminded Jane of a Viking, simply took the entire bowl.

When Sheriff Moore reached for a sweet, Fiona slapped his hand away. "Your doctor said no desserts."

He grumbled under his breath, and the dear woman rolled her eyes.

"All right, everyone," Jane announced. "Now that you've warmed your bellies with cookies, it's time to head outside."

"Okay to bring Cheddar?" Conrad asked.

"Of course."

After he'd leashed up the sweetheart, they headed to the reflection center, where a circle of stone benches waited. In the spring and summer, this area was ablaze with color from the gorgeous green of the wisteria to the white, pink and blue gardenias that bloomed to perfection and filled the air with the sweetest scent. But tonight, stars twinkled overhead in a pitch sky. Moonlight glistened from tree limbs, making each appear glazed with silvery snow.

Eight hand-woven wicker baskets filled with metal candles with LED bulbs waited on each of the stone benches. A ninth basket contained eight candles made of wax. Cold yet somehow toasty warm and fuzzy, Jane swept her gaze over the small crowd. Everyone dressed to the nines, wearing their winter best. They were smiling. Happy to be together. A family. Team Truth.

A soft blanket of satisfaction spread over her. When her gaze lingered on Conrad, the sensation heightened.

*The end comes...*

The thought drifted through her mind, igniting a flame of dread. Nope. Not going there. Fear wouldn't ruin this moment.

"You okay?" Beau asked her softly, approaching her side.

"I am." Better than. "How about you?" They hadn't really chatted much since Thanksgiving, both on the go more than usual. "How's Sora?"

He pursed his lips. "I think it's time to get started, yeah?" he asked everyone.

Cheers arose, an irresistible call to Jane. *Good play, Harden. Good play.*

"All right, then." She reached into the basket with wax candles and lifted a thick pillar high in the air, catching the attention of the group. Conversations lulled. "When gold was first discovered in the nineteenth century, men and women from around the globe flocked to this area of Georgia, bringing their traditions with them. Among them was a group from Finland, so very far away from home, but who asked to light candles to remember those who had passed, connecting the living with those they'd left behind. A small piece of their birthplace here in their new homeland. This very spot is believed to be the place where that tradition began in the Garden."

A gentle wind whistled through the bare limbs of the trees, as if welcoming the tradition for another year.

She passed the basket around, allowing everyone to select a wax candle of their own. Then she passed the rest of the baskets around, ensuring everyone received one. That done, she lit Conrad's wax candle to her right, and Beau's candle to her left. She watched, awed, as fire flickered to life for one person after the next. Soon the entire circle glowed.

"As you leave the reflection area, keep the wax candle with you but place the LEDs anywhere you'd like. Tonight, the grounds are yours to explore. If you feel so inclined, speak a blessing over those who have passed before us as well as their families. This is our Christmas gift to them."

As they moved forward, Fiona's lovely soprano filled the night, the moving lyrics to Silent Night adding to the solemnity of the moment. Soon candlelight flickered in every direction, the cemetery coming to life. From the slow chirp of the crickets, to the gentle rustle of the winter grasses and the hoot of resident owls.

"May those you left behind and those who came after you always find and follow the light in the darkness," she whispered to one and all.

Her ears twitched when Conrad issued a whispered blessing of his own, but she failed to make out any word but "love."

When the group crested the berm, her breath caught. The sight below stunned her. Hundreds of LED candles glowed. More than light, they represented love and hope. All because of a small circle of people.

Circle.

The circles Benjamin had drawn in his notebook. The anagrams he'd encircled. What was she missing? What, what?

*Circle, circle.*

*Drip, drip.*

AT 3:16 in the morning, Jane jolted upright with a gasp. Something inside her screamed the treasure could be found inside the circle. But where was the circle?

Excitement hit as she flipped on a light and studied the map with her markings. Hmm. No matter what angle she used, no circle emerged. Disappointment set in. Until she remembered the map from the library. The original map of the grounds. What if it differed from the map she held... which differed slightly from the map in the mausoleum?

She snatched her phone and keyed up the photos she'd taken. During a thorough search of every section, she began to grow disappointed again...until she reached Paradise Ladling. Jane sucked in a breath. There. In the original map, there'd been only one caretaker's cottage. The home she now lived in had yet to be built. Paradise Ladling had extended into this acreage. And yes, Silas and his family had been buried here. At some point, however, someone had moved the first family closer to the other Ladlings, freeing this space.

With Silas's original gravesite instead of his current one, the seven names on Benjamin's list formed a full, perfect circle. In the center of it was...drum roll please...the bridge between Autumn Grove and Eden Valley.

Did X mark the spot? Was she soon to discover a cache of gold?

Heart thundering, she scrambled out of bed while Rolex watched. Phone in hand, Jane shoved her feet inside winter boots. She yanked a gorgeous winter hat with faux fur ear muffs onto her head, slung a scarf around her neck, and thrust her arms into a coat. If Conrad wasn't out and about in the cottage, she wasn't going to disturb him. Yet. Not until she had—or not—the gold.

She swiped up her flashlight, sporting a delightful red and green handle perfect for Christmas, and exited her room as quietly as possible. Downstairs she went. Through the back-door and into the cold, breath misting in front of her face. Light on. No sign of Conrad.

Another spark of disappointment, but onward and upward. Knowing these beloved seventy-five acres forward and backward, side to side and upside down, she rushed along short cuts, reaching the mausoleum in record time.

Flashlight aglow, Jane hastened to the bridge. Made of aged stone and brick, with two thick arches rising over a dry creek bed. Shored, thank goodness, and safe. She climbed down the hill with ease to study the underside of the bridge. As a child, she used to play beneath these arches. In fact, she'd practiced hosting funerals here. She remembered tracing her fingertips over circles carved in the center of the inner arch.

She examined each one and... yes! Just as she remembered, each bore a series of grooves, but only one...three... five...seven stones had smooth, circular centers. She grinned.

Were the stones loose, perhaps? Get them out of the way and find a cubby hole under the bridge?

She set the flashlight at her feet, freeing both hands. When she pulled, nothing happened. When she pushed with all her might...biceps burning...yes! The stone moved at last, a musty smell escaping.

Invigorated by her progress, Jane kept at her task but dang it, she made little progress. She needed some muscle. Time to wake up her roommate-boyfriend. She phoned Conrad.

"Jane?" he asked with a sleepy tone. "Everything okay?"

"Come to the bridge and bring your biggest muscles. We're about to find out if there's a secret stash of gold!"

"You broke the code?" Rustling sounds filled the line.

"I did."

"Bafflingly smart," he muttered.

Her heart clenched. 'Baffling smart' had been one of his girlfriend requirements. "You can gush about my amazing brilliance later. Hurry or I go in alone!" Click. That should motivate him to hustle.

Within only a few minutes, he reached the bridge, calling her name.

"Down here," she responded.

He descended, using his cell phone as a flashlight, and joined her at the wall, somehow more gorgeous than ever. Like her, he must have thrown on whatever was closest, which just happened to be gray sweatpants, combat boots, a sweatshirt proudly pronouncing: Don't Be Cryin' Vote for Ryan. "A gag gift from Wyatt," he muttered when he noticed her stare.

She fought a grin. "You see those seven stones?" she asked, pointing with the flashlight. "I think they'll move with the right amount of force."

Conrad's whole body strained as he shoved his weight into the jagged rock. When nothing happened, doubt settled heavily over her shoulders. Maybe she was wrong. Maybe she'd woken up her boyfriend and dragged him out here for nothing. Then, it happened. The slow, grinding sound of rock sliding against rock filled her ears. Such a lovely music. The first stone inched backwards.

Grinning, she jumped up and down. "You did it."

"I did something at least," he said, excitement tinging his voice. The remaining six rocks weren't as stubborn as the first and shifted much more easily. A pattern emerged in the jagged stone…a doorway?

He blinked. "Is that what I think it is?"

"Maybe? Keep going!"

Her heart hammered against her ribs as he slammed the side of his body into the rock. She helped as best she could, pushing and pushing. Oh, oh! It moved! They shared a triumphant smile. He hit it again and again and she pushed until some kind of crank took over. Chains rattled, and they both stumbled back.

The door jerked to the side of its own accord, creating

enough space for someone to walk through. Also enough space for the scent of earth and decay to seep out, tickling her nose.

"It *is* a doorway," she exclaimed. A secret entrance to a secret space! Was the gold inside? "We did it!"

"*You* did it."

Yeah. She kind of did. She chewed on her bottom lip. "Um, it would be dumb to go inside, right?"

"Or dumb not to," he said.

"Yes! That one. Dumb not to. Exactly what I was thinking. Because we've finally done it. We can't really turn back now."

"Also because I need to know what's inside." He moved forward. "You can look after I make sure it's safe."

"Fine. Deal. Yes." Anything!

He paused and held out his hand. "Give me your flashlight. And your scarf."

She unwound her scarf without hesitation. "Why do you need this?"

He wound the fabric around the lower part of his face. "Just in case." He eased past the entrance and stopped, shining the light forward.

"Do you see anything?"

"A mound of stones, but nothing else." He paused. "No animals or bugs scurrying about. I'm taking that as a good sign."

"Stones?" Could gold be underneath?

Conrad eased back and removed the scarf. He tapped the flashlight's handle along the sides of the stone frame. No debris fell to the ground. "All right. Your turn. You get a quick in and out," he said, untying the scarf and winding it around the lower part of *her* face.

"Thank you, thank you, thank you," she exclaimed.

"By the way, I'm going in with you. Ready?" he asked, offering his hand.

Jane's answer was to link their fingers and start forward.

They entered a small four by four space with thick darkness and musty air that at one time must have been used for storage under the bridge. She jerked her beam back and forth.

*C'mon baby! Light momma up some gold.*

Then her beam landed on the mound of stone he'd mentioned. She stepped toward it. Jane startled when she spotted what lay behind it. Withered remains dressed in men's clothing. Beside him lay a journal in brown leather, exactly like the one Benjamin had used and an old-fashioned lantern, the inside of the glass darkened with soot.

Still at her side, Conrad groaned. "Negative on gold. Positive on this being a potential crime scene."

# CHAPTER TWELVE

If your heart gets to drumming, my darling, you should get
to listening. You might just hear the wedding march.

–Lily Ladling's Holiday Advice for Ladies Cursed in Love

*J*ane hated to admit it, but she liked watching
Conrad slip into Special Agent mode.

"Don't touch anything," he said, sighing as he
eased forward. He crouched before the body to study it more
closely. The dead man wore pleated trousers and a brown
suit jacket with a sharkskin weave and flapped pocket. A flat
cap lay on his thigh.

Conrad used the tip of his cell phone to crack open the
journal. "If I'm reading the faded handwriting correctly, this
belonged to Opal Ladling."

Great grandmother Opal had kept a journal too?

"Conrad, that body must belong to my great Grandfather
Benjamin. The writer of my journal. Well, his journal. He

went missing, remember? But how'd he get trapped down here? The door isn't rigged to close on its own." Oh! "I bet Elise Dansing stole the gold and shut him in."

"No. If he were entombed alive, he would have eaten the pages of the journal. Someone put him in here dead or dying." Conrad continued flipping through the journal. "There's only one passage. The rest of the pages are blank. Come over here and see if you can decipher the handwriting."

Jane joined him in front of the body, crouching beside him to scan the page. A story unfolded. Wow, wow, wow. "My dearest Benjamin," she read. "To put the kibosh on your tomcatting, I found you a new place to live. Since you stole my dignity, I took your gold."

"So there *was* a treasure," Conrad said.

"Mmm hmm. Seems like. Opal went on to say that while Benjamin was trying to decipher the code, she was doing the same."

Basically, the woman had made it a matter of finders keepers. "She left Benjamin the journal so he'd know he could've had an amazing life with her, but he'd earned an agonizing death instead. You're right. She spiked his whiskey that night and used a wheelbarrow to whisk him to his living tomb. He was alive but dying when she locked him up."

Wow, wow, wow, Jane thought again.

"Great grandma Opal was hardcore," Conrad said, ushering her outside. "Do you know what this means? The Ladling curse didn't kill Benjamin. His wife did."

Jane's jaw went slack. That was…it wasn't…she could… maybe, possibly…?

"Despite the holiday and the timeframe, I've got to treat this like any other potential homicide and call it in." He straightened with a sigh. "GBH will send out agents. They'll take the body and run tests. After they confirm your ancestor's identity and year of death, the body will be released to you for burial."

Jane forced herself to concentrate. "I'm not sure Benjamin will want to claim his spot. It's next door to Opal." Although, if two people had ever deserved each other...

Just as the sun peeked above the horizon, a team of GBH agents arrived. She recognized most of them; especially the tall woman with the dark bob. Special Agent Karen Hightower. Annoyance radiated from the woman.

Hightower had never really forgiven Jane for being a mystery solver rather than a murderer.

"I know you're all eager to get home to your families," Jane called, remembering the damage done to her beloved bushes last time, "but please be careful not to trample over mine as you traverse the Garden."

As Conrad predicted, the investigators looked around and asked questions. Jane ventured back and forth from cottage to bridge, passing out cookies and mugs of the marshmallow cream hot chocolate she'd whipped up. At some point, two men wheeled the deceased away. The other agents sectioned off the area with crime scene tape.

"This isn't how I imagined our first Christmas together," Conrad told her, slinging his arm around her waist to tuck her into the warmth of his body.

"It's much better, though, right?" A centuries-old mystery had been solved. Benjamin was no longer trapped with his guilt. And defeat. The presence of gold had been established. Though where Opal had hidden it presented another mystery, didn't it? Or had she lied simply to crank up her husband's misery? Because the woman sure as heck never spent it.

The corners of Conrad's mouth twitched. "Much better." A pause. Then, "In your complicated mind, what does this mean for the Ladling curse?"

"Honestly? I'm not a hundred percent sure yet. Family legend claims it originated with Silas's daughter Evangeline. Maybe that's a mystery we can solve next Christmas."

A slow smile bloomed. "Next Christmas it is, then."

Eventually, everyone else departed, leaving Conrad and Jane alone at last. They strode to the cottage hand-in-hand. Inside, she could only gape as she scanned the living room. Broken Christmas tree ornaments. Shredded toilet paper lay strewn across the wood floor from one side to the other. Piles of the stuff topped the kitchen table, and spanned atop the couch, near Cheddar, who lay with his snout resting on his paws, his eyes round and projecting a message: *It wasn't me.*

"What happened here?" Conrad asked, clearly trying not to laugh.

"Can't you guess, officer? Rolex wanted us to have a white Christmas." The fur-baby sat on the coffee table, a ribbon of tissue stuck to one of his fangs. "Such a sweet darling."

"Sweet. Yes. That is, in fact, a word." He kissed Jane on the lips. "Meet me back here in twenty minutes? I have a present for you."

A gift exchange! Though she wanted to insist they get started right away, she nodded. Twenty minutes was just enough time to race through a shower and change into clean clothes.

Heart thrumming with excitement, and dang it, giggling like a schoolgirl, she flew into her bedroom to rush through a shower. Being with Conrad was certainly better than being without him. But what gift had he gotten her? And would he like the gift she'd found for him?

She was practically bubbling over by the time she donned a delightful Christmas vest, a handcrafted gift from Fiona and headed downstairs with thirteen seconds to spare, gift in hand. A laugh burst from Jane when she spotted her boyfriend. He'd showered, too, and changed into worn jeans and a plain white T-shirt that read "Curse Breaker."

Could this man be any more perfect?

He'd even had time to clean up the mess and ignite the logs in the hearth. Golden firelight gave the space a magical glow. He held a thin rectangular box gloriously wrapped in white Japanese chiyogami paper with gold polka dots embellished by a gold bow and a miniature bell.

When she stood before him, their eyes met, and he smiled.

"For you," she said, holding out the gift in her hands. Midsize, square and wrapped in a map of Aurelian Hills. "Merry Christmas, Conrad."

"Merry Christmas, Jane." He offered her the box he held.

"Ready, set, go," she cried, and they both laughed as they tore into the packaging.

Inside a bed of tissue, she found a nameplate with roses etched along the edges, and gold lettering across the center. *Jane Ladling, AS, MM, FMR*

She traced her fingertips over the length of each engraving, her eyes watering. He also traced his fingertips over his present. A plaque bearing the words: *Sheriff Conrad Ryan. Bad Guys Don't Stand a Chance.*

Again, they grinned at each other. But this time, there were all kinds of emotion in the undertone.

"Looks like we had the same idea," she said. "But what does the AS and MM and FMR stand for?"

"Amazing Sleuth, Miracle Matchmaker, and I'm not going to tell you the last one yet. I'll know when you're ready."

Oh, she loved it so much more! But what did he mean, he wasn't going to tell her? She must know now, now, now. "First Mystery Responder? Forever Miss Risky? Fated Mate Regulator?"

He snorted. "You aren't even in the ballpark, sweetheart."

With a flourish, he produced another present, tucked beneath a pillow on the couch.

"What? There's more? That's wonderful because...I have something else for you, too." She raced to the kitchen and tugged open the cabinet beneath the sink and pulled out a second gift.

Joining him, she stared down at the packages they held. Both wrapped in matching brown wrapping and stamped with The Treasure Room, the premier showplace for the crafters of Aurelian Hills.

"Oh, I can't wait a moment longer," she told him, her nails ripping into the paper before the final word left her lips. Jane gasped when she spotted two pictures in a frame. The first was a candid shot of Rolex looking at her with absolute adoration. Directly below that was a selfie Conrad had taken with Cheddar and Rolex, who glared at her boyfriend with murder in his beautiful eyes. Adorable.

Her throat tightened and she blinked quickly to ward off tears. "Three of my favorite men. Okay, you open yours."

With a grin, Conrad tore into his package. He smoothed back the tissue to reveal a frame. Instead of photos, it was a map of Aurelian Hills. His new home in the Palisades was circled with a line hand drawn ran across the map, leading directly to her cottage.

"So you'll never lose your way," she told him.

The muscles along his neck worked as he gazed at the map, then his focus shifted to her. Hunger and need and love for her blazed in his amber eyes. "Never."

His single word was a promise and her bones nearly melted. She hugged the frame he'd given her to her chest. For too long, she'd lived in fear. Afraid of falling. Afraid of loss and heartache. She had denied her heart what it craved most: to love and be loved. Meaning yes, she had absolutely cursed herself.

Tears welled in her eyes, and okay, yes, a few droplets even streamed down her cheeks. But no more. From now on, she rejected fear. In fact, a new year kicked off soon. Jane would be making some changes. Big ones. Want different results, do something different.

Conrad cupped her jawline and brushed away her tears with his thumbs. "I'm glad we're back together."

A lump grew in her throat, but she swallowed it back. "Me, too. I missed you even though you were living in my home."

His lopsided smile made an appearance. "You did?"

"I really, really did."

"By the way, this is my favorite Christmas." He wrapped his arms around her and lowered his head. She slid her palms up his chest and rose to her tiptoes. Their lips met in the middle for a sweet kiss.

"Just wait till the next one," she said. Despite her determination to fight fear, a blip of it surged to the surface. If she lost him before then...

No. No! He was all in. And so was she.

"I'm not going anywhere," he promised her. "You mean everything to me, and I plan to prove it to you."

Okay, yes. She chose to believe him rather than the fear; Conrad wasn't a liar. The fear just might be. "Conrad," she began. "I–" What? What did she wish to tell him? Words poised at the end of her tongue, but her mind couldn't yet decipher them. In the end, she just fisted his shirt while tears of happiness streamed down her cheeks.

"I know," he said, wiping away the droplets and covering her mouth with his own.

# EPILOGUE

*I*, Rolex the Great and Mighty, Sultan of Fang and Fury, stalk a slow circle around the intruder as he attempts to steal my servant queen's breath. This, after he made those awful water droplets seep from her eyes! This man and his infernal mutt have caused us nothing but trouble for too long.

Forget my plans for the day. There will be no napping. No snacking or destroying the annoyingly bright feathers growing from my favorite ball. No coughing up an irritating hairball on Miss Jane's bed or shattering a vase that has taunted me with its shine for weeks, just begging to take a tumble to the floor.

The time has come to make the interloper regret his birth. I will use him as a scratching post. Slap his ridiculous face until his brain rattles against his skull, and hiss until he curls into a little ball and sobs for mercy he shall not receive. He won't walk away from me—he'll crawl.

I must—gah! The long bodied orange and white slobber goblin dared to touch his paw to my newest ball of yarn. My vengeance must be swift!

Cattain Rolex, signing out to take care of business.

Ready for Conrad Ryan's side of the story? Look for:
Conrad: Falling For the Gravekeeper
March 27, 2023

**Books in the Jane Ladling Series**
Romancing the Gravestone
No Gravestone Left Unturned
Game of Gravestones
Twelve Graves of Christmas
Conrad: Falling For the Gravekeeper

**Books in the Writing Fiction Series:**
All Write Already
All Write Already Workbook
The Write Life
Write Now! An All Write Already Journal

# ABOUT GENA SHOWALTER

Gena Showalter is the New York Times and USA TODAY bestselling author of multiple "unputdownable" series in paranormal, contemporary, and young adult romance.

Learn more about Gena, her menagerie of rescue dogs, and all her upcoming books at genashowalter.com

# ALSO BY GENA SHOWALTER

**Immortal Enemies**

Start with: Heartless

.

**Rise of the Warlords**

Start with: The Warlord

.

**Lords of the Underworld**

Start with: The Darkest Night

.

**White Rabbit Chronicles**

Start with: Alice in Zombieland

.

**Tales of an Extraordinary Girl**

Start with: Playing with Fire

.

**Everlife**

Start with: Firstlife

.

**Original Heartbreakers**

Start with: The Secret Fling

.

**Angels of the Dark:**

Start with: Wicked Nights

.

**Otherworld Assassins**

Start with: Last Kiss Goodnight

.

**Gena's Complete List of Releases:**

GenaShowalter.com/books

# ABOUT JILL MONROE

Jill Monroe is the international best selling author of over fifteen novels and novellas. Her books are available across the globe and *The Wrong Bed: Naked Pursuit* has been adapted for the small screen for Lifetime Movie Network.

When not writing, Jill makes her home in Oklahoma with her husband, enjoys daily walks with her dog Zoey, texting with her two daughters who are away at college and collecting fabric for items she'll sew poorly.

Learn more about Jill at jillmonroe.com

## ALSO BY JILL MONROE

**Sworn Series**:

Sworn Promises

Sworn Duty

Sworn By A Kiss

Sworn Protector

.

**Wrong Bed Series**

Naked Thrill

Naked Pursuit*

*(Now a movie from Lifetime Movie Network)

.

**From Hallmark:**

At The Heart of Christmas

.

**Spicy Romance:**

Fun & Games

Treasure in the Sand (novella)

.

**Jill's Complete List of Releases:**

https://jillmonroe.com/allbooks/

Made in the USA
Middletown, DE
01 November 2022